Praise for Jo:

Country

"... characters that jump right off the page ... [as] a demented, lascivious and murdering trucker goes up against a crafty, middle-aged P.I. ... realistic portrayals which will have you biting your nails ..."—*T.L Barrett, coauthor of Hairy Bromance and author of The Night Library.*

"Hirsch is an astonishing talent who, with muscular writing, has created in Aaron Neblett a genuinely scary, and very human, psychopathic killer. *Rolling Country* is a real page-turner—with both absolute depravity and surprising humanity on full display .... I like the surprise ... the suddenness and finality of [the ending] was more satisfying and real to me than the Vegas 'Top of the World, Ma!' moment that I envisioned."——*John Sheppard, author of Small Town Punk and Tales of the Peacetime Army.*

"Aaron Neblett will suck you into the first chapter and refuse to let you go. This is a book you won't soon forget ... even though you'll want to."—*Dawne Dominique, author of the award-winning First series.*

"... well done and well-written... the ending ... is great and unexpected and original."—*Cetwya Powell, filmmaker and publisher of Underground Voices.*

Also by Joseph Hirsch

War-Crossed Eyes

Ohio at Dusk

Orphan Elixir

House of Crystal

ROLLING COUNTRY

Joseph Hirsch

Moonshine Cove Publishing, LLC

Abbeville, South Carolina U.S.A.

This book is a work of fiction. Names, characters, places and incidents are products of the author's imagination or are used fictitiously. Any resemblance to actual events, locals or persons, living or dead, is entirely coincidental.

ISBN: 978-1-937327-25-5

Library of Congress Control Number: 2013941200

Book design by Moonshine Cove; original cover art by Dawne Dominique, DusktillDawn Designs (http://dusktildawndesigns.com/)

For

Cetywa Powell

About the Author

Joseph Hirsch served four years in the U.S. Army, and was stationed in locales as exotic and disparate as Baghdad, Iraq, Darmstadt, Germany and El Paso, Texas. He was honorably discharged in 2008 and he never looked back. He previously wrote columns for *Fight Hype,* covering boxing matches around the globe. In addition, he has also sold short stories to *3AM Magazine*, *Underground Voices*, and *Zahir: A Journal of Speculative Fiction.* He has published two previous novels, *Ohio at Dusk* and *War-Crossed Eyes*, as well as two novellas, *Orphan Elixir* and *House of Crystal.* He currently lives in Cincinnati, Ohio, where he is attending the University of Cincinnati on the Montgomery GI Bill, and majoring in German Studies. He has a dog named Tiffany, a half-Terrier, half-Chihuahua mix hellion. Previously, he was a finalist in a Glimmer Train Short Story Award Competition for New Writers.

Rolling Country is his first novel published by *Moonshine Cove.*

For information and updates, visit the author at:

www.rollingcountry.com

http://www.amazon.com/JosephHirsch/e/B00CJEECZY/ref=ntt_athr_dp_pel_1

After you kill someone, anything is possible

— *Roy Demeo*

If youth only knew; if age only could

—*Henri Estienne*

ROLLING COUNTRY

Chapter One

The two men agreed to meet on the El Paso side of the border, at a small storage facility in the valley. One of the men, Jefe Ayala, was already inside, waiting. The other one, Aaron Neblett, was parking his sixty-foot rig in front of the gate outside of the storage facility. He put the truck in park, and then he got out and chocked the wheels. Aaron Neblett then headed for the compound.

A massive pylon hung above the storage facility, on top of which was a bit of lollipop-shaped signage where an astronaut floated above the Sierra Madres, blotting out the garish hyacinth and tapioca shanties nestled among the carrizo on the Juarez side of the border. *Space Station,* the sign said.

Neblett resituated the revolver in his belt and then entered a code into the numeric keypad on the face of the black gate. A green LED light flashed twice, and the gate rolled open. He walked inside. To his left there were rows and rows of storage lockers, with their corrugated steel faces drawn shut. To the right there were more of the small garages, all of them shuttered. Jefe Ayala waited in front one of the lockers, leaning against its metal face.

Jefe used his hand as a sun visor, squinting. He recognized Aaron Neblett, and waved. Neblett did not wave back, but instead walked forward to meet the small Mexican man. Aaron Neblett was six-foot three, a hulking man with tinted prescription glasses and a red beard that melted into his shoulder-length hair, which, when contrasted with his scarred and ruddy skin, made him look much more like a biker than a hippy, someone whose only interest in drugs was in selling them, not in using them to expand his mind. He wore a satin powder-blue jacket covered in patches, and his head was topped by a mesh-webbed trucker hat.

Jefe Ayala smiled, showing a tooth inlaid with a golden starburst, which caught a splash of yellow light bleeding down from the sun which flowed across the cloudless South Texas sky. "Hola, *carnal.*"

"Hola," Neblett said, deliberately pronouncing the "H" at the beginning of the word. "What you got for me?"

Jefe held up a small finger and nodded. "Something good." He stuck a key into a padlock on the face of the storage locker, and threw the rolling door upward until it disappeared. The storage locker was empty inside, except for a small woman huddled in the far right corner of the room. Her face was pressed against the wall and she held her wrists in front of her mouth.

"Mira!" Jefe shouted. He then yelled something at her in rapid-fire Spanish. Neblett understood only small snatches of Jefe's speech. The girl turned slowly. Her skin was dark red, almost vermillion. She was young. Her large brown eyes were deep and terrified, and there was a metallic strip of duct tape wrapped across her mouth.

Jefe Ayala and Aaron Neblett stared at her. Neblett spoke first. "Does she speak English?"

"Doesn't matter," Jefe said. "She is pretty much deaf." He wiped sweat from the back of his neck with a dirty blue bandana, and then wadded the cloth into a small ball. "Some boys down in Sinaloa got her from Chiapas. They fired guns next to her ear to make her behave. Maybe they did it one too many times." He shrugged.

The girl attempted to stand, and fell over into a small puddle of her own urine. Her hands and feet were bound together, the wrists tied to the ankles with flexi-cuffs. "Where do you want her?" Neblett said.

Jefe went into the breast pocket of his Guayabera shirt, which was crawling with a thorn-like ivy pattern that blossomed at the shoulders into rose-shaped epaulettes. "This address...." He handed the piece of paper to Neblett. "Careful on the way, *carnal.* They got those machines can see through your truck."

"Not my truck." Neblett took the piece of paper, folded it, and put it into his back pocket. "Drogas?"

"Si," Jefe said, walking forward, deeper into the storage locker. The girl writhed, but was too weak to do much moving. Ayala lifted the girl's tan blouse, exposing her stomach, each of the six muscles like a tight rock. Jefe Ayala patted her belly, which responded with a fleshy thud. "Aqui," Is it a problem?"

"No problemo. Those gamma machines they've got at the checkpoints won't pick her up. The trailer's a reefer, so she'll stay cool."

"Bueno, then," Jefe said.

"Bueno. Dinero facil," Neblett said, again speaking in his peculiarly unaccented Spanish. "I guess this is a COD job?"

Jefe nodded, and kneeled. He ran his blue bandana across the girl's bruised and sweating face. Her raven hair was caked to her temples, wrapped by grit and moisture around the curve of her ears. The whites of her terrified eyes were now almost the size of eggs, swimming in untold agony. "Ten-thousand." Jefe held the blue bandana to his face. He smelled it and smiled. The girl looked at him as if she wanted to spit, prevented from consummating the act by only the duct-tape covering her mouth.

Aaron Neblett suddenly removed the .38 Taurus from his belt. He pointed it at a stunned and confused Jefe Ayala, who took a dum-dum round to the solar plexus before he could even raise his hands in protest. The round mushroomed inside of his body and escaped through his back, spitting bits of tissue and blood-wrapped bone onto the walls of the storage locker. The unnamed girl watched Neblett walk over to the downed man. Ayala's left hand was open, while his right fist closed and opened spasmodically. The truck driver stayed the right hand with his work boot and fired two more shots into Jefe Ayala's blood-soaked chest and stomach. Wisps of smoke spilled from the snub-nosed barrel of the gun, and another cottony length of blood-misted hot air wafted from the dead Mexican's chest.

The girl's eyes watched Aaron Neblett, briefly flitting over to the dead man's body before roving back to the hulking white man who held the gun. Air escaped from her nostrils and the tape over her mouth writhed. Sweat trickled down her scalp. Somewhere a shell rattled along the ribbed aluminum wall of the container.

Aaron Neblett walked around behind the woman and emptied the three remaining chambers of his revolver into the back of her head, firing in quick succession, catching her with each shot, raising her body with the pneumatic force of the bullets, which jerked her upward each time she attempted to fall forward.

The truck driver then walked to the front of the storage unit and pulled the door closed, leaving him and the two bodies to sit in darkness. The meaty, sour smell of blood comingled with the earthen smell of the dirt which had been preserved in the cold confines of the storage locker, creating an odor not unlike that of a dank basement with leaking pipes. After about five minutes, Neblett touched the barrel of the gun with his hand. It was cold enough. He replaced the revolver in his waistband and stepped out of the shipping container, closing the door as he left.

He walked between the rows of shuttered metal doors. A pickup entered *Space Station*, coming through the gate and pulling forward, a white Ford F-150. The driver, a bald and squat man in suspenders, saw Neblett and waved. Aaron waved back, and the man headed left, down the dirty gravel corridor.

Neblett walked back to his rig, a white truck with a fiberglass Cabover face, attached by a series of pigtail cables to a white trailer. The trailer was emblazoned with a red depiction of a very wooly bison, somber and wreathed in a kinky brown mane. *Nebraska Meats Co.* the truck said.

He hopped up into the cab, using three points of contact. He climbed across his leather seat, and grabbed a small key which hung from a hook attached to a shift pattern diagram. He glanced quickly at the indicator light which was nestled between the driver and passenger seat. The cycle indicator showed that the refrigeration unit was still in its freeze cycle. He had been doing this so long that when the engine was running, he could quite literally *hear* what cycle the thing was in without even bothering to look. He grabbed a garbage bag from among the miscellaneous tools and trash in the floorboards. Then he hopped down from the truck with his little key in hand, and walked to the back of the cab.

He stood before the cab guard, which was nestled between the exhaust stacks sprouting from either side of the tractor. Hopping on top of the exposed apron of the fifth wheel, he inserted his key into the keyhole. He opened the door to the secured locker and extracted a knife with a scythe-like blade. He dug into the First Aid kit inside of the headache rack and removed a pair of latex gloves. Throwing everything into the trash bag, he relocked the box before heading back to the storage facility.

The sun was now at its apogee, pulsing, broadcasting a nuclear signal of impending doom that made its victims understand why men had once worshipped it. Neblett walked back down to the storage locker where he had been busy moments before. He went inside, closing the door behind him. Pulling a small pen light from his pocket and turning it on, he held the light between his teeth and slid the latex gloves over his hands until both responded with satisfying snaps.

Neblett dug his knife out of the trash bag and worked in the half-light. Placing the blade a couple of inches above the dead woman's pudendum, he ripped upward with all of his considerable force. Her stomach relented with a gaseous rip, the fat and subdural layers yielding as a spicy, warm scent filled the confines of the small room. He fished around inside of her stomach, poking with his fingers, sliding the cold latex of his gloves among the cramped warm organs as they sloshed and crowded around his hand. He found the organs sensuous, their heavy and intimate contours making him both sick and excited.

Almost nothing made his heart beat like this, he noted, studying himself from the cold distance where he watched everything, even his own actions. Killing the little Mexican man had not made him feel happy. This did, though.

After several minutes of rooting around, guided only by sense of touch, Neblett slowly came to distinguish between what was her, the vital tissue that was warm and had pumped with her life, and what was not her, what were in fact the double-layered condoms which had initially felt so much like something that had been part of her body. The little elusive slugs obstinately slipped around his grasp. They were covered in his sweat, her blood, and the loose feces from a colon that had been pierced by his errant blade.

He found eighteen of the condoms in all. There may have been more, but he was tired and his knees hurt. *Kneepads,* he told himself. He needed to add kneepads to all of the safety paraphernalia he had accumulated, the useful tools like the grease gun and the warning cones that he kept in either the cab guard, or in the tractor cab proper.

He pushed the dead and useless body away from him and removed his shirt. After sliding the gloves off of his hands, his palms slimy from the heat, he wrapped the gloves and the knife inside of the shirt. Then he bundled the flannel shirt into a ball and put it in the garbage bag and gathered the bloated latex worms and threw them on top of the shirt.

He shone his flashlight over the ribbed, V-neck undershirt he now wore. It was white, with only a couple of bloodstains, so faint that it would have been easy for a state highway trooper to misconstrue them as hot sauce.

Aaron Neblett left the storage container, padlocked it, and walked back to his refrigerated truck with the trash bag in tow.

It was dusk, the cinnabar red mountains and hills now dark and indistinguishable from the brown basin below. There was a chill to the air. The drastic shift in temperature always came as a shock to his system at that moment when the sun finally set and ceased to define the desert. Aaron Neblett shivered, looked left and then right. He was satisfied that he was not being watched, and he headed to one of the 150 gallon-capacity gas tanks on his truck.

He removed the false bottom and stuffed the garbage bag inside. Then he replaced the false bottom and headed back to the cab. He opened the door, hopped inside, turned the key in the ignition, and gave the diesel engine a moment to come to life. He could hear the reefer unit groaning, even over the sound of the engine. It wailed behind the riveted bulkhead at the front of the trailer. His instrument panel glowed. The light cluster came to life. His QUALCOMM blinked, greeting him like the sentient little monster he believed it to be. He had grown to know and love it. He tapped the face of the computer with the stylus attached to the tablet required to check and confirm cargo, and to report overages, shortages, and damaged goods.

There were no new messages. He clicked the "Daily Report" tab and wrote the last few hours off as "routine preventative maintenance." He then turned on his *Galaxy* two-way citizens band radio which was plugged into the lighter socket, and he cued the power on his ruggedized laptop. There was very little light, but the computer was designed to work in less than optimal conditions.

"Got one," someone on the CB said. Neblett recognized the voice. It was a fellow Nebraska Meats employee down here on a similar mission. "You got a what?" Someone else asked.

"Osprey," the first voice said.

"Bullshit," the other voice said. "You don't know your ass from a hole in the ground, so don't expect me to believe you know an osprey from a cormorant."

Birdwatchers, Aaron thought distastefully. He turned his CB down a bit, and was happy to see that the laptop was ready and standing by to divert him. He selected his playlist and pressed play: "I Can't Drive Fifty-Five," by Sammy Hagar filled the glowing confines of the humming cab. Aaron Neblett whistled, and pulled out of the drive in front of *Space Station.*

There was a steamy hiss, and the exhaust stacks whispered darkly, as if they were blowing piping hot brimstone through the holes in their perforated metal tubes. The trucker drummed his hands on the steering wheel.

This was going to be cinch, he told himself. The only hard parts about trucking could either be done by a yard hostler (like coupling the tractor and trailer), or they could be avoided altogether (like parallel parking). All he had to do was stay awake while he drove. It was pretty simple, and fun.

For now, the priority was to press north on I-25. There was a nice little motel along that stretch of road that went by the name of Beaut-E Rest motor court. It was located in one of those little out of the way no-name towns between Las Cruces and Truth or Consequences, New Mexico. It would take him a bit more than an hour to get there if he kept the hammer down. He would get a little food, a little sleep, and maybe even a little bit something else later on.

Chapter Two

El Paso's highways were a series of rebar and concrete wound in interlocking figure-eight patterns staggered above and below one another, forming a series of convoluted over-and underpasses more complex and annoying than anything seen outside of Los Angeles proper. It took Aaron Neblett more than ten minutes of navigating before he found himself pointed north on I-25, heading for Las Cruces.

Marty Robbins was singing on his little hardened computer, serenading the cab with his tale of heartache along the border. His El Paso bore little resemblance to the city that Neblett had just left, which was not a romantic backwater of cantinas where men staged gunfights in their claims for the hands of fair maidens, but was rather a series of ugly yardarm advertisements for *Denny's* and *La Quinta* arrayed in bland repeating patterns, interspersed with sickly neon that advertised second-rate motels. Their noxious glow polluted the foothills of the distant Sierra Madres, there on the other side of a tattered border fence which offered no more opposition than a floodwall.

"You think you got problems," someone groaned on the CB radio. "I'm hauling forty-five thousand pounds of Budweiser. Try telling them that at your next AA meeting."

Short cacti stood in the dark at either side of the road. Oncoming trucks dimmed their high-beams and Aaron returned the favor more than once. Absently gripping the turn signal stem in his left hand as if it were a dumbbell, flexing his grip around it and then letting go, he fell in behind another rig, a double-decked lowboy hauling Toyota Camry four-doors on its trailer bed. He previously heard a story regarding those trucks while shooting the breeze on the CB, about how allegedly the keys were left in the ignition of those cars, and that hoboes who used to ride the rails now preferred to sit high in the sky, basking in the warm comfort of heated Corinthian leather and draining the batteries as they listened to some baseball on the a.m. radio and made their way across the country. Neblett didn't know whether or not it was true, as he had never driven a lowboy hauling cars. He had never driven anything besides reefers and dry vans, in fact. He didn't mess with flatbed trucks (or "skateboards" as the boys back at Nebraska Meats called them), since they usually had to be tarped down, and tarping a rig was a hassle. Even when a man took his time tarping the load down, he was as liable as not to get pulled over by some pencil-dicked DOT agent who would find a way to fine him.

"Name of the town's Weed," someone on the *Galaxy* CB said. "They can't keep the sign up. Pothead kids keep stealing the frigging thing."

Someone on the channel laughed, a scratchy guffaw that was half the result of a lifetime of smoking, and half the result of the crackle that accompanied any sound too loud to properly carry across the radio.

Aaron Neblett kept one hand off the wheel, and took his cellphone down from where it was clipped to the visor above his head. This act required all of his strength to keep the rig on the road. The Kenworth had power steering, but one of the steer tires felt low and a degree of camber was beginning to creep into the wheel. He set the cellphone down and used his right hand to cue an internet browser window on the on-board computer. He deftly used his index finger to pull up bookmarks and selected the top one, the one with the gold star next to it. It said:

"Eros Kitten: Las Cruces Adult Services-Transsexuals-Chocolate Thunder."

There was a five-image thumbnail gallery of Chocolate Thunder, a mocha-colored transsexual with a beauty mole. She wore black fishnets with lace garters clipped to a red teddy that matched her lipstick. Over that, she wore a crimson blazer, which was held open to display ample but obviously surgically-enhanced cleavage. She wore tortoise-shell glasses and bit the expensive ballpoint pen she held between her lips. She was seated in a swivel chair with her legs spread apart, and the overall impression she gave was of a dutiful secretary finally ready to cross the threshold with a boss who had been asking her to work late night for the last week or so, a man who had been too timid to outright ask for what she was now prepared to give him. Aaron Neblett read the telephone number listed beneath the picture gallery, and he dialed. The line rang twice, and she picked up.

"Hello?" She sounded groggy.

His heart leapt in his chest, and he had to move his mouth away from the phone in order to draw in a breath, lest he reveal the excitement in his voice, and frighten her with his obsessive devotion. "Chocolate?" He could not have said her whole name. He would have been embarrassed to say it out loud. "It's me, the big old trucker. We met at Beaut-E rest."

"Oh, Papi." Her voice was hoarse. "You got to let mama get her sleep. I have to catch a flight to Vegas for the Adult Video Awards in the morning. You know?"

"Chocolate, please. I'll give you another two-hundred. Just, please." His legs were trembling. He almost let his left hand fall from the wheel, but reclaimed it just before the jittery wander in steering pulled him right off into the dust and the dark horizon of green cacti dancing in the blackened night beyond the lights of the road.

"Baby, I got to catch a flight." There was a note of finality in her voice. "Next time...."

He heaved a sigh so heavy that his sternum touched his red beard. "Next time," he finally conceded. His half-erection tossed in his pants, and his prostate grew wet at the thought of her touch. They hung up by silent, mutual accord.

Minutes later he was pulling into the Beaut-E Rest motor court. The lobby was at the tail end of the building. Planter boxes filled with wildflowers bookended the entrance, which, like the rest of the building, was made from ashlar dressed stones. Aaron Neblett set the brakes, changed his duty status on the log to "off-duty," and then chocked the wheels with the block.

He walked toward the lamp-lit entrance of the lobby. A bell dinged as he entered. Two faux wooden logs were burning in a gas-lit fireplace whose visible blue jet ruined the effect. A custodian relaxing between his rounds played chess against himself on a table in front of the fire.

Aaron Neblett went to the front desk and greeted the proprietress. "Long time no see," she said. She brushed a Siamese cat away from the counter and brought an old-fashioned credit card reader from behind the desk. Neblett went through his wallet, his gas cards good at participating fueling stations, with any number of showers and amenities accrued after so many fuelings, and he handed his credit card to her.

Aaron opened the large ledger on the face of the desk, while she was swiping his card. A gilded bit of typewriter ribbon held the place on the guest log. He thumbed through the pages and found his entry from a previous stay, his looping curlicue signature and the date separated by hyphens. He turned ahead in the book to the next empty space, and with the pen attached by a chain to the book he printed his name in block letters, provided a couple of strokes for his signature, and then he wrote the date. He closed the book, took his receipt from the woman, and thanked her.

He smiled, a painfully bright expression held on his face for the briefest moment, and gone the next. He walked back outside into a lightly falling drizzle. The parched desert gratefully received the water, and the parking lot was now obsidian black, slick and reflecting the orange light which peeked out from the curtains drawn across each of the rooms in the motel. Aaron went back to his rig, and he removed the garbage bag from the false bottom of the gas tank. He slung the bag over his right shoulder and headed toward the laundry room, following the dull hum of fluorescence, one industrial chant among the many in this motel, a constancy not unlike the glowing ice machine and the industrial air-conditioning units, all of it soothing, but somehow nowhere near as placating as the drone of the refrigerator unit of his truck. It had been his companion for many miles (over one-million safe miles achieved), through many years of this dedicated route, back and forth, from North Platte, Nebraska down to Las Cruces, New

Mexico, with occasional stopovers in El Paso- for women, for drugs, for guns-and sometimes all three (what Jefe had called "triple plays").

He found the laundry machines out of order. Someone had taken tape and crisscrossed it in a dense web over the coin-op slots. Several signs were posted saying "OUT OF ORDER" written in black marker. The room had fallen into general disuse besides that, with lint traps scattered across the floor and a bit of standing water in one corner of the room, where a dead spider floated in a brackish puddle. Someone came in the room after Aaron Neblett and looked at the trucker for a moment.

"She's out of order," Neblett said.

"Shit," the other man said, turning to leave.

Aaron Neblett walked out of the laundry room and headed to the door whose number matched the one on his pine-cone shaped keychain. He inserted the key into the door and entered. The floor was plush oatmeal shag, tall enough to almost bend leeward like grass in a light wind when the AC was on this high. The curtains were slatted, and pattered softly against the glass window. Aaron looked at the quilted down blanket covering the bed, and imagined leaning over, his palms gripping the diamond-shaped patterns of the bedspread as he took all of Chocolate Thunder, accommodating nine inches of her manhood.

His heart sank again, lurched like the brakes on his rig when the slack adjusters were misaligned. He tried not to think of it and turned on the television. The boob tube was good for drowning out thoughts. John Wayne was on, in all of his black and white glory. The only person who looked better in the vampire's perpetuity of eternal reruns was good old Rod Serling, whose eerie *Twilight Zone* would continue to exist as long as man and his most prized possession, television, held out.

Aaron Neblett turned the volume up, and he listened to the stock musical strains gush as John Wayne galloped through Monument Valley, appointed with its buttes and mesas and fat-bellied clouds. Neblett stripped until he was completely naked. His chest and belly were covered with a soft layer of downy black hair. His single tattoo was an anchor-and-globe on his right forearm, commemorating his time in the Marine Corps. He would sometimes flex, stare at it in the mirror, and hum a couple of lines about Montezuma and Tripoli.

He turned on the hot water tap of the shower, fished the double-wrapped condoms from the garbage bag, and placed them in the tub.

A watery admixture of feces and blood were flushed from the outer layer of the latex sleeves, swirling around the drain in a bilious pool of compromised reddish-brown that resembled nothing so much as the texture and color of a child's water colors after they were all hastily combined. After Neblett was certain that the excess fluids from the Mexican woman's stomach had been rinsed from the condoms, he set them out on the floor mat to dry.

Everything else had to go, he decided. He would keep the condoms, hiding them in the gas tank or maybe in the headache rack, but the rest of it-the bloodstained shirt and the knife- would be buried in the dumpster in the morning. The world was big, its roads, highways, and towns affording a complex anonymity that, when added to the general indifference he had observed in so many people, pretty much ensured that no one would be able to pin those two bodies in the storage locker on him. He had no priors, no traffic citations, not so much as a moving violation. And even if they somehow did attach his name to the crime, he mused as he sat on the edge of the bed and watched the Duke, the prospect of prison did not frighten him.

It meant time to read, and free meals guaranteed into the foreseeable future. He had an uncle who did time all over California, at Chino and at Folsom, going all the way back to a juvenile stint at Deuel Vocational School for Boys. He fell asleep naked there on the edge of the bed, dreaming of triple-stranded concertina, interlaced with barbed wire, massive guard towers looming below cottony white clouds that covered the sky thickly.

***

In the morning, he dressed, wrapped the condoms in a towel, and then carried them out to the false gas tank, where he hid them. He rushed to throw the rest of the garbage bag's contents into the big industrial dumpster located behind the motel. He then returned the key to the day manager of the Beaut-E Rest, a man Aaron believed to be the husband of the woman who worked the desk at night.

His delivery was not due until 9 a.m., but he had to hurry if he was going to make it to Tio's for their breakfast special. He drove there quickly, pulled his rig into one of the parking spaces which faced a series of anthropomorphic tacos who smiled at the customers and stood adjacent to large plastic menus. Speaker boxes were nestled into the center of the tacos' faces. Each of the corn tortilla shells wore black top hats, and held fancy canes in their hands.

"What'll it be?" A teenager's puberty-wracked voice came from the little dancing taco's mouth.

"Breakfast burrito! With the Pico de Gallo and the sopapilla, too!"

"Coffee?" the Taco asked.

"Sure as shitting. No sugar, no cream."

"Eight ninety-five."

Aaron whistled dramatically at the price hike and took out his wallet. He cursed himself for forgetting the menudo, which always came with steamy strips of white tripe nestled in among the beans. He tended to eat only once per day. Lots of guys kept their cabs filled with snacks, but he preferred to drive on an empty stomach. It kept the mind sharp. He found that driving on a full stomach was almost as dangerous as having a few brews and a handful of pills before hitting the road. He knew guys who did that, too, took "handlebars," "red tops," "yellow jackets," and all manner of stimulants and depressants, uppers and downers, to keep themselves going.

Something else to consider was that nothing started a fire like a pile of trash, with the possible exception of a lit cigarette on the floor of the cab. Enough *Slim Jim* wrappers floating around inside the Cabover, pressed up against a heating vent, with maybe a little bit of antifreeze leaking in, and anything could happen, especially to the guys who drove the hazmat trucks.

A kid in a paper hat arrived with his food and he paid for it, taking it over to the picnic area. The table was located underneath an umbrella shielding him from the waking sun, a merciless Aztec orb that pummeled oases to dry alkali and reminded him that as a white man, he was in the wrong place, no matter what the hell went down in Santa Ana a long time ago or how much he slathered himself with Coppertone. He hated the Southwest, loved the Plains States. He enjoyed driving in the Midwest and he was partial to New England (except for some of the tolls). The only two places he would never drive a rig again were Oakland, California and West Memphis, Arkansas. The odds were better for the Duke riding his palomino solo through Apache country, than for a white man with several-hundred thousand dollars' worth of cargo cruising by his lonesome through the City by the Bay.

Most guys agreed that New York City was nowhere near as bad as its reputation. The bridges provided amazing vistas, steep drops into the gray chopping waters of the Hudson. The sidewalk pavement was invisible from the number of people crawling over it. The bicycle couriers weaved expertly in and out of one's path, playing hell on his convex mirrors, but it was somewhere worth seeing at least once, and maybe even more than once.

Aaron finished his sopapilla, devouring the fried pocket, its honeyed glaze lightly dusted with powdered sugar that dissolved on his tongue. He scalded his mouth with the breakfast burrito, the chile peppers peeking from between the fluffy eggs. He put that fire out with the icy salsa, hinted with lime and swimming in the Pico. After wrapping all of his trash into a wad and throwing it into a wastebasket next to the table, he hopped back into his rig.

On the CB, the current squawk was about which routes had been declared off-limits for big rigs since 9-11. "Hoover Dam," someone said. "You ain't driving anywhere near there these days." Neblett had heard rumors that Eisenhower Tunnel and Vail Pass, both in Colorado, had limited their access in the wake of the terrorist attacks, but he didn't want to add his two cents to the conversation if he wasn't sure. Besides that, he preferred to listen rather than speak.

The Perdue Wholesale Distribution center was a gray fortress, carved from the seemingly same stone that had once been used to sculpt gargoyles for the protection of German cathedrals.

It looked as if it could have withstood anything that might have conceivably been measured on the Richter scale, and was in actuality more foreboding than many a prison. Its position in a gully between two residual hills divorced from the Sierras proper made it seem more like a secret missile defense silo than a simple meats distribution wholesaler.

Aaron pulled up to the gate, handing his ID and a hardcopy manifest to a guard seated in his pillbox. The guard radioed news of Aaron's arrival to the interested parties, and then handed the trucker his ID and clipboard back. "Proceed to dock nineteen."

The candy-striped arm lifted from his path and Aaron drove forward. His rig groaned, and the refrigeration unit churned behind him. He drove over the slick concrete, hitting puddles which had formed sometime last night after the obstinate drizzle steadily increased until it was a righteous downpour. The rain had ceased just as senselessly as it had begun after only a few minutes of torrential spasms.

The foreman and several workers were already on the dock. The metronomic beep of a forklift wailed through the cavern of the massive warehouse into which the dock receded. Aaron watched both of his mirrors as he backed up, making sure that the dock was equidistant from either side, and that he had the same view in both mirrors. He continued backing up slowly, waiting for the slight bump to register in his cab, that feeling that was so similar to the one he felt whenever the fifth wheel correctly mated with the kingpin, in that drawn-out ritual known to all truckers as the coupling of the tractor and trailer.

A mild shock, a subcutaneous tremble, went through the Kenworth's massive frame, and he set the brakes. He grabbed the tablet and stylus from the passenger seat of his cab and he hopped down. After walking around to the back of the truck, he climbed up the ramp to the dock.

The foreman ran a barcode scanner over the banded seal on the back of the truck, and then gave one of his dockworkers a slight nod.

The worker took out a pair of pliers with a mean set of steel teeth, and he tore the band from the back of the truck. He then stepped away, and two other strong-backed workers slid the rolling door of the truck upward. A frozen gust of sparkling cold air flooded out of the trailer, like a banking wind of dry ice. The men coughed and stood aside. Aaron was used to it. He held the stylus and tablet out to the foreman, who was a scarecrow of a man, as large as Neblett but less muscular. His steel blue eyes had the distant, harried cast of a man who had more responsibility than he wanted, but probably needed the extra money to pay down debts he would never entirely settle.

"Nothing like the smell of bison in the morning," he said as he signed the tablet and handed it back to Aaron.

"Give me a home where the buffalo roam," Aaron replied.

Both men stood aside for the mewling forklift headed their way. It was a yellow mechanized monster, a bug whose feelers reached out for the pallets which the dock workers eased onto its steel tines. "What's the difference," the foreman asked, "between buffalo and bison?"

Neblett shrugged. "Same thing, pretty much. Just different words, I guess."

The foreman watched the workers load a stack of cardboard boxes onto the forklift. He shook his head in disbelief, and spoke to his men as they heaved boxes. "I don't know who eats this shit. What's wrong with a burger?"

Neblett watched the men as they worked. The steel load locks which braced the cargo hold were covered in a thin layer of wet, seeping hoar which dripped onto the floor of the tractor trailer and collected in cold pools. Enough crates had already been removed that the soggy molting wooden dunnage was visible on the floor. When neither of the workers answered their foreman's question, Aaron answered for the both of them: "They say bison's about the leanest red meat there is."

Chapter Three

The detective scattered the stack of coffee-stained essays across the passenger seat, the glaring examples of passive voice and the instances of "hisself" or "should of" making him grateful to have this time off from teaching. It wasn't the students he minded, really; it was just their god-awful writing.

He found what he was looking for beneath the stack of paper-clipped homework assignments, which were now strewn across the floorboards, and he took the lancelet in his hand. He pricked his index finger and applied a bit of blood to one of the test strips he selected from a small pile in his cup holder. He then threw the lancelet back onto the passenger seat and held the bloodied test strip in one hand, precariously balancing it as he snatched his Glucometer from the dashboard, where it had slid flush against the front windshield.

He inserted the test strip into the Glucometer and waited. A moment later, the digital readout gave his blood sugar as a solid 200. He grimaced. He would have to stop and get something to eat after this. The detective threw his diabetic accoutrement onto the passenger seat, turned the key in the ignition, and then headed toward his client's house.

462 Boniface was one among many tract houses in the neighborhood, all built in the optimism of another age, and now languishing in various stages of disrepair. This home was far from the worst on the block, the detective observed, but its vinyl siding (and even the Saint Francis lawn ornament) could have used some maintenance. As the detective got out of his car, he noticed the curtains in the front window of the house part, as a butterscotch cat claimed its perch on the windowsill. The cat's eyes watched him as he got out of his late model Ford sedan and walked up the driveway.

The detective pressed the doorbell once and waited. Behind him, a boy rode by on his bike, wobbling from side to side as he attempted perhaps for the first time to pedal without training wheels. The boy threw a rock at a nearby warped, rusted Neighborhood Watch sign as he flew past the detective on his bike. The sign rattled once, before growing still.

The front door opened, and a large woman in a nightgown stared at Detective James Arklow from behind the worn, slightly torn screen door. "You the detective?"

"Yes, ma'am."

"One minute...." She opened the screen door, averted her head, and coughed as he entered. "Come on in."

Inside the house smelled like cats, the odor of their fur as well as the smell of their droppings overpowering whatever weak lemon or pine treatment had been sprayed to mask their feline musk. There was also the smell of cigarettes, probably an off-brand, as well as that indeterminate smell of ribbon candy combined with mothballs that was always associated with the aged, just as embalming fluid was associated with the deceased.

"You want to have a seat?" She asked.

"Sure." There were two glider chairs, one with the legs retracted and one with the legs extended, facing a TV nestled in a cabinet. The television was tuned into *The Price is Right,* with the volume turned down. Bob Barker held his trademark thin microphone out to a woman. She had a waddle of fat beneath her chin, and was using the "One Dollar" method to bid on a set of golf clubs.

Detective Arklow took the chair with the least cat hair on it, the one with the legs retracted. The cat, perhaps sensing the detective's squeamishness, came down from the sill and coiled into a ball at the head of his chair in order to better irritate the intrusive human.

"You want something to drink?" The woman's voice came from the kitchen.

The detective leaned forward in his chair. "Whatever you're having, madam."

"Madam!" She shouted, obviously bridling at the term. "I ain't running a damn whorehouse. Though sometimes it sure felt like it."

Detective Arklow thought of apologizing, or perhaps explaining to her that "ma'am" was merely a contraction of "madam," but he let it go. He was not here to give grammar lessons, and she was clearly feigning offense in order to break the ice. She came back into the living room a moment later, carrying two nearly tulip-thin glasses filled with cold iced tea.

"Thank you." He accepted one of the glasses in his hand and took a sip. He rocked back and forth in the glider, and felt the vibration of the cat's purr as it reverberated through the chair.

"Amy couldn't turn a stray away." She made a purring sound and patted her lap, entreating the cat to come sit. The ever-defiant butterscotch kitty decided that was its cue to move, but not in her direction. It stood and hopped off the chair in one balletic motion.

James Arklow drained half of his glass in one swig. It was usually best to wait a few minutes before getting into the case, but Margaret Loeher had broached the subject of her missing daughter, and now was as good a time as any to start. He wiped the condensation from his glass of iced tea onto the crease in his khakis. "Have the police released any information to you, Mrs. Loeher?"

"Maggie." She reached onto the glass table in front of her and grabbed a pack of Virginia Slims and a green Bic lighter, from where they were resting on top of an open *National Enquirer* magazine.

"Maggie. Well, then, you can call me 'James', not 'Detective Arklow.'"

"That was my plan all along." She lit her cigarette. She made a pained expression and blew a side stream of smoke from the crook of her mouth. "Formality's a waste of time for me at this age."

He knew that she was only in her fifties, but he also knew what she meant by her comment. There was weariness in her face, croissant-like bags beneath her eyes, crosshatches and weather-beaten lines drawn by nature, that sadistic artist, who intended to demonstrate with his quill how harsh in fact time could be. Detective James Arklow saw it all written on her, and knew that while her daughter's disappearance might have been a mighty blow, it was only one in a long succession of them. The pain preceding the loss of her daughter could have been caused by anything; an abusive husband, or father, or brother; a cherished boyfriend killed in Vietnam, or in a car accident. Something had happened before this, whatever it was, he knew.

Detective Arklow returned to his question, or rather silently waited for Maggie Loeher to return to it. "The police won't release anything," she said, and smoked. "It's one of those catch twenty-two things. The only way I can get them to release anything is if I agree to let them close the investigation."

"And you won't do that?"

She rocked in her glider chair, briefly glanced at *The Price is Right.* The woman on TV gave the wheel a mighty spin. Various numbers flitted by the little red needle that clicked and made blipping noises, until the wheel came to rest. "I can't tell them to stop the investigation. It would hurt my heart too much." She looked at the curtain covering the one window in the room, blotted with light from the sun that filtered through the glass. "But maybe I should tell them to close the case. That way at least they would have to release some information to me, and then I could give that to you."

"It's ultimately your call." He had the urge to check the smudged drinking glass he held in his hand for cleanliness, but didn't want to offend her by holding it up to the light and inspecting it right then.

"They're useless." She shook her head, disgusted. She ground her Slim out in the ashtray and fished in the pack for another one. "They were going to dredge the lake, but they said there wasn't enough money in the department's budget to buy a sonar machine. Then," Maggie Loeher closed her eyes and shook her head. She paused, and her lips trembled. "They said if her body was in the woods, hunting season was coming up and someone might find it."

"I would like to see what they have. I'm sure the lead agency has her telephone records. I would certainly like to see those."

They were quiet for a moment, only the low *whap-whapping* of a ceiling fan working above them, and the tinny scurrying of a moth trapped inside of a light-bulb, fluttering in panic as if it was performing one-half of a desperate mating ritual alone.

"Amy Loeher was reported missing exactly one year and two days ago," the detective said. "By you." He finished his iced tea. He set the glass down with a satisfied exhalation. "That was when you called the police. Correct?"

Mrs. Loeher opened her eyes. "That's correct." She pulled in the legs of her glider, put her half-smoked cigarette in the ashtray, and leaned forward to face the detective. The months which had turned into a year led her to believe that this was all hopeless. The detective didn't seem to think so, and it momentarily reassured her. "I don't think the cops cared. Amy was a drug addict, and she was a frequent flyer."

"Frequent flyer?"

"It means she was in and out of Juvie."

"For what?"

Maggie retrieved a half-smoked cigarette from the ashtray. Detective Arklow watched her as she smoked. He had smoked Marlboro Reds with no filters years ago, and though he had given up the habit, watching her smoke the relatively weak Virginia Slims was as maddening as watching someone try to drink a fudge brownie through a straw. Why, he asked himself, did only older women smoke the damn things when they required the lung capacity of Paul Bunyan to even garner a decent pull?

"She got caught panhandling a couple of times, outside of a McDonald's, and she liked to run away."

According to what Mrs. Loeher initially told the detective, Amy had been seventeen and only a couple of months away from her eighteenth birthday when she disappeared. Even if she hadn't been a drug addict, the police were less likely to get excited about a near-major disappearing, rather than a twelve year-old. The people needed a narrative, and an Amber Alert with a fresh young face, a smile absent a couple of baby teeth, drew more sympathy and hotline tips than a young adult who liked to do dope. Amy was relatively young and blond, but the "missing white girl syndrome" that Detective James Arklow taught his students about only went so far.

"Anything else?" The detective said. "Any other reasons she went to Juvie?"

Maggie Loeher inhaled deeply, and her eyelashes fluttered. *Here it comes,* the detective thought. "She got caught stripping at a topless and bottomless joint off Route Sixty."

"Do you know the name of the place?" The detective removed his notepad and pencil stub from inside of his front left pants pocket.

"Bare Sensations." Maggie Loeher stood and took the detective's empty glass. "I'll get you some more tea."

She left the room before he could protest. He stood and walked to the doorway separating the kitchen from the living room. The kitchen was a preserved kitsch artifact from the 1970s. There was a honeycombed linoleum pattern on the floor, and a smooth-edged refrigerator that probably pumped out enough CFCs to singlehandedly melt the ozone layer. There were stainless steel wraparound countertops. For a moment, it was easy to imagine that he was home early from the office, and that his hausfrau was dutifully making him a highball as she asked him about his day.

The illusion was shattered as Maggie let out a loud rasping cough. She reached for a half-smoked pack of cigarettes nestled in her spice rack, as if they were the cure rather than the cause of her spasms. James Arklow wanted to hug her, to hold her. She reminded him of someone's mother or aunt, a woman who had sacrificed whatever meager ambitions she had ever held, all for the sake of someone else who had eventually had forsaken her, the "who" inconsequential.

She handed him another glass of tea. He mouthed the words "Thank You," and then said,

"Mrs. Loeher, what kind of drugs was your daughter into?"

"I caught her snorting something once. She said it was Ritalin, but I don't know."

"Did she have any friends?"

"None, not after whatever friends she had started a whisper campaign about her at church. After they found out she was dancing, they began talking bad about her and she stopped going to services."

"Did she keep a diary?"

Mrs. Loeher laughed for the first time that day. "When she went in for her GED, she got a perfect score on her Math and her Science, but when it came time for her to do the writing portion, the question was in essay form. 'Give an example of goal-setting' was what it said. She left it blank and ended up failing the test. She didn't much like to do writing, you see."

Mrs. Loeher absently twirled an unlit cigarette and the detective shook the glass of iced tea he held in his right hand, making the cubes clatter as he swirled the glass back and forth. Both of them were thinking, she of her past, and he of the case. The detective looked down at the floor, the blurring paraffin of the waxy linoleum catching light from the bulb that dangled naked from the ceiling.

"Did she work?" he asked.

The girl's mother laughed again. "I was a full-time job."

"What do you mean?"

She held up her hands, and for the first time he noticed how gnarled they were, how the fingers curved like whittled twigs, the knuckles like reddened knots of sore putty that were melting under pressure. The digits were involuntary retracting inward like prehensile claws. "Carpal tunnel, one-hundred percent disabled. I do background checks from home, but sometimes I have to do my little ergonomic exercises, and she would help me with those."

"What do you do now that she's gone?"

"I have someone come in once a month to do little flexion stretches, and massages. They're very good at it."

"Do you go out much?"

"This is as far as I go." Maggie Loeher headed out the back door. Detective Arklow followed her outside. The yard was hemmed in by a wooden fence, the unvarnished planks interspersed with brick accents. The grass was high enough to almost hide the pointed red hats of the Bavarian garden gnomes nestled in the grass like daemonic kobolds, waiting for their chance to spring to life and attack their human warders.

There was a birdbath in the center of the yard. Two cherubic stone angels sat on the concrete lip of the bath and looked into the center of the bowl, their downcast eyes fixed upon the font that was now empty of water and filled with moss. At the far end of the yard there were two tiny crosses painted in whitewash, like the ones found at the shoulders of highways intended to commemorate roadside DUI fatalities.

"This is where I come to relax," Maggie said. She lit her cigarette, took a drag, and waved a cloud away from both her own face and that of the detective.

"What are those?" Arklow asked, pointing to the two little crosses.

Maggie pointed with the hand not holding the cigarette. "The one on the left is Mr. Butterworth, a gerbil, and the other one is his wife, Mrs. Butterworth." Mrs. Loeher wobbled on unsteady legs, and almost fell into Detective Arklow. He steadied her and led her over toward a pair of rusted lawn chairs. Both of the chairs were covered with a thin layer of moisture from the recent rain.

She leaned on the detective, placed her head into his clavicle, and burped. He caught a whiff and it was clear that her previous iced tea was of the Long Island variety. "Mr. Butterworth beat his wife into the grave by about six months. His wife died from a broken heart shortly thereafter." She burped again. "She was crestfallen." Maggie closed her eyes, and passed out.

Detective Arklow set his iced tea down onto the little bit of concrete pad visible between the brambly tangles of crabgrass and weeds competing at his feet. He propped Mrs. Loeher up in one of the lawn chairs. He removed the Virginia Slim from her hand and surprised himself by taking a drag.

A plane rent the naked blue sky above them. He watched it tear through the azure sheen and leave a trail of rippled white exhaust in its wake. The detective's pilfering of her cigarette brought Maggie back to full consciousness just as quickly as she left it. "You smoke?" She asked.

"I did. But I quit years ago."

"Then give me that." She pulled the cigarette from his hand and placed it in her mouth. She puffed without taking a break, squinting her eyes as the smoke made them water, curling her nose, huffing like a steam engine. A moment later she gave up on the odd drunken charade and switched back to smoking conventionally again, using one of her two arthritic hands to hold the cigarette. A dog barked from an adjoining yard.

"Forgive this mess," she said. "I have an old push mower, and there's no way I could make any headway with my hands all messed up." She waved her cigarette toward the weedy, knee-high expanse of sickly untended green thicket, and she inadvertently ashed her Virginia Slim as she waved it like a wand.

"It's okay. I can cut it for you if you want."

She shot up in the chair. "You would?"

"I will," he said, standing. "Tomorrow."

He helped her struggle to her feet and led her back into the house. "For now, I'm going to let you get some rest, because you're no good to me like this. And I'm going to set myself up in the Extended Stay downtown, get settled in."

"I'll write you a check, in the morning. Just let me know about incidentals, expenses."

"Don't worry. This is my sabbatical time. I'm rusty and I need to prove to myself that I can still do this. And anything is better than grading more of my students' papers." He led her up the stairs, aware that she was semiconscious and that he was now talking only to himself. "I need a new case to talk about with my students, anyway."

Maggie Loeher burped again. "Don't use my real name." She said, sputtering. "Names are protective innocence… or somebody…maybe the cat ate it."

"Okay." He led her over to her glider in the living room and extended the legs fully, then laid her in the chair. He took the Afghan quilt from the headrest behind her and stretched the cat hair-infused blanket across her chest and lap. Her chin was now resting on her left shoulder. She moaned in her sleep. The sun was lowering in the sky outside of the window, and the light had dissipated from the curtain which had previously captured the day's radiance. It was dark in the house, and in the dimness it was possible for James Arklow to see her as she was twenty years ago, before she'd given birth to a daughter who would torture her by first making her care, and then by not caring quite so much about herself. The detective was grateful, for the moment, that he had never had children. That momentary gratitude was, however, contradicted by a preceding decade's worth of agony which had probably contributed to the messy divorce from his wife, Janine. His Azoospermia, the doctor informed him, was amenable to treatment, but after a few years he became convinced that no amount of "looser underwear" or "avoidance of bicycle riding" could counteract his wife's ceaseless nagging, and during the course of their worst arguments he suspected that Janine's ball-breaking manner was literally the culprit in causing his low sperm count.

He searched in the dark on the coffee table, fumbling among the Virginia Slims and the *Enquirer* whose open pages reported on the state of the English Royals, and the cellulite of not-ready-for-the-beach American celebrities photographed unwittingly in a series of voyeuristic poses while sunning on the San Tropez beach. He had the idea that he could find the remote control for the television, turn the volume up on the game shows to perhaps help her sleep, drown out whatever dreams might intrude on her.

His pursuit was interrupted by a mad pipe organ, startled to life by the cat who had taken it upon itself to stride across the Casio keyboard in the corner, triggering a preset version of "Asleep in Jesus."

He walked over to the keyboard, which was braced against a low mantle where several photographs were arranged. The first few framed pictures were of Maggie Loeher when she was a teenager. There was a grainy color photograph, the rich tones of a Kodak picture reminding him of the garish bright colors of Super 8 home movies. In another photograph she was beaming in a prom picture, betraying no sign in her expression that she knew what the years ahead held for her. The smile on her face was bright, and her corsage was blue. There was a picture of her as an "Employee of the Month," many years later. She was basking in a moderate amount of silly string shot by fellow coworkers, while another two held up the banner proclaiming her victory.

The other couple photos were of Amy Loeher. In one of them, she was an eight or nine year-old girl, wearing a conical birthday hat and crouched in front of a party magician who made a wiener dog from lengths of balloon, while she looked on and blew a noisemaker. The next photo was of her as a teenager, much closer to what she looked like now.

Her hair was corn blonde, almost bleached, and her skin was equally pale, giving her the impression of a beautiful yet fading apparition. Detective James Arklow searched her eyes with his own, and though he always tried to find some spark, especially in a victim so young, it was somehow plainly evident to him, however he arrived at these intuitive conclusions, that the girl was not especially bright. She could perhaps read people very well and survive on the streets, but even at the age of sixteen (or approximately thereabouts) something was already gone from her.

He suspected that she hid much from her mother, and that even though he had more questions for Maggie Loeher, he would not get at the heart of what he needed to know about Amy's disappearance by asking the mother a bunch of questions.

Still the pictures served a purpose, and if Maggie had any photos somewhere of her siblings in their early twenties, those would be especially helpful in anticipating any changes that late pubescence might bring about in Amy's facial structure, since her appearance could have changed much in the time she had been gone, especially if she had a growth spurt. This was of course assuming she was in fact on the run (or had been kidnapped), and was not at the bottom of a lake or out in the woods somewhere, waiting for a pack of deer hunters or a budgetary increase that would allow the police to purchase a sonar device which might find her body deep in the water, and grant her arthritis wracked mother some surcease. In the good detective's experience, the age-progression software that police departments used had as many limitations as traditional sketch artists. Family photos were the best and cheapest form of age progression that money could buy.

Sometime during his study of the photos on the mantle, the pipe organ auto-play version of "Asleep in Jesus" segued into an ersatz Hammond organ version of "Nearer My God to Thee." The cat was nowhere in sight, and Maggie was snoring. The detective reached into his pocket for his little notepad and removed the pencil stub from where it was secured in the spirals. He began to write beneath "*Bare Sensations on Sixty*:"

"*Ask where the father is...*"

"*Ask about boyfriends...*"

He tapped the soft lead of the pencil against the paper. He knew he was forgetting something. "Ah," he said out loud, and wrote:

"*Cut lawn....*"

He closed the notebook and walked outside, shutting the door behind him. The street was quiet, the golden hour in its final minutes before the sun slumbered as surely as the old woman who lived at 462 Boniface.

Chapter Four

The yard hostler at Nebraska Meats was someone who prioritized new tattoos over groceries, if his skinny ink-covered frame gave any indication of his state of mind. His bare arms were an India ink tapestry of flaming eyeballs and dagger-pierced hearts, with some scrollwork devoted to "Mom," "Lenore," and even a nod to Jesus. Aaron Neblett stepped down from his rig and let the boy take over.

"She's all yours," he said.

There was nothing to worry about. The eighteen condoms were now in an oversized Ziploc baggie in the locked guard of the cab. The hostler would drive the Kenworth over to the mechanic's bay, have Cephus give her the onceover, and he would then take her through the pressure washer, having it ready for Aaron later today. Aaron would go check in with Dispatch and then head home for some much needed shuteye.

"Ain't you cold?"

Aaron turned to the questioner. It was Clem Roundman. He looked like Johnny Paycheck at his lowest ebb, back when he was headed to Chillicothe prison. He was standing under a shade tree, holding a red invoice in his left hand. "You get fined?" Aaron asked, walking over and nodding at the piece of paper in his fellow over-the-roader's hand.

Clem looked down at the piece of paper. "This? Goddamn, my EZ pass usually gets me through the weigh station around Grand Island, but for some reason this time she goes red instead of green. I pull in, DOT does me a level three, and I come in over on steers. Two-hundred and fifty dollar fine." He whispered the last part. Aaron let loose a commensurate whistle.

"I feel your pain brother."

"Yeah, you really want to feel my pain, you'd go halves on this fine with me."

"What's in it for me?"

"Neblett!" Someone behind him shouted.

"I'm Mr. Popular today." He spun. Clem gave him a parting wink. Aaron Neblett walked over to Rhonda the dispatcher. She held the front door to Nebraska Meats open. She wore a short fireball-red beehive, and streaks of her matching lipstick ran off onto the massive wad of gum she chewed.

"Hey, Rhonda." Most dispatchers tended to hide out behind bulletproof glass. More than anyone else, they controlled the livelihoods of the drivers, played God by deciding who got the good routes and who got the crap ones. They could be as vengeful as the Old Testament Yahweh, bumping a driver from a plum route for doing something as justifiable as taking a day off for chemo treatments. Aaron had been doing this long enough to have witnessed a driver follow a dispatcher home and set their house on fire, in retaliation for what the driver perceived to be a series of deliberately bad routes.

Rhonda had escaped that fate thus far, and was even well-liked by most drivers. Part of what allowed her to come out from behind the bullet-proof glass was the fact that she was generally random with her assignations (aside from with those who had earned dedicated routes like Neblett), but a lot of her status as a free-range dispatcher was owed equally to a latent sense of chivalry among most of the drivers. Burning down a man's house was one thing; disrespecting a woman was quite another.

"What you want?" Aaron asked, playfully.

"I don't want nothing. I got to get back to my post and give Miley's dumbass directions on how to do his recaps, which means I don't have time to play with you. Skip wants to see you upstairs, though."

Aaron walked into the massive warehouse, an echoing hangar of crossbeams and transoms. He greeted the air raid-like sounds of forklifts as they let out warnings when backing up, the hiss and crackle of someone welding in another part of the building, and the PSI pump of a pressure washer splashing against hard metal grates. Nebraska Meats was a massive hive, cast in the dark light of fluorescent tubes smudged with grease and creosote.

Neblett thanked Rhonda, who then returned to her Plexiglas pillbox with the Qualcomm satellite equipment and cameras (on which she probably previously spotted him dicking around with Clem underneath the shade tree). Aaron climbed the cold steel steps, holding the guiderail as he made his way up the catwalk.

The Skipper's office was a room whose walls were built from thin plywood, and whose ceiling was made from the same tin as that of the massive Quonset hangar. It was a freestanding improvised fort, as flimsy as a teenager's tree house, not necessarily what one might think of when trying to imagine the node of this whole operation.

"Just come on in!" Skip shouted.

Aaron wasn't sure exactly how he had been made, but he opened the door. The office was small enough that he found himself in front of the vinyl swivel chair facing Skip's desk the moment he entered. "Monsieur Neblett..." Skip said. He leaned back in his chair.

Skip Blaincock looked like Elvis might have, had he survived the Seventies and lived long enough to let himself really go until he was indistinguishable from his plethora of impersonators. His hair was slicked (with Vaseline, pomade, or perhaps even monkey grease) from pompadour to ducktail, and the patterns on the ties he wore looked like they were lifted from a book of wallpaper swatches.

It wasn't that Skip Blaincock had no style. It was merely that he committed himself very hard to being in season one year many years ago, and hence decided that he would remain in that year through the passing decades. He favored short-sleeve shirts with his ties, which gave him the impression of being either a Jehovah's Witness or a door-to-door vacuum cleaner salesman, and there wasn't an inch of his forearms that wasn't covered with a thick layer of downy black hair.

"Aaron, you were a devil dog like me, weren't you?" Skip picked up a piece of paper on his desk and began reading. "You can sit down if you want."

"Yes sir."

Mr. Blaincock waved away the show of deference, telling Aaron with his gesture to dispense with the title. He then pointed at the seat across from his own. Mr. Neblett sat down. "I only ask because when I was in the Marines, we had a saying. Or at least my old gunny sergeant had one. Or two...." Skip Blaincock suddenly huffed, as if enduring a bout of indigestion. When the moment passed, he spoke again: "Around here, the squeaky wheel gets replaced." He laughed, showing nacre-white dentures, the buck teeth glowing like Chiclets.

Aaron smiled. Laughing at the boss's jokes was a painless form of ass kissing, but he feared it might get worse. "The other saying: 'Every good soldier gets one Article Fifteen.' You ever hear that, Aaron?"

"No sir. I mean, Skip."

"Well, what it means is that a man who's never been in trouble is a man you can't trust. You believe that?"

Aaron thought for a moment about what answer Skip may have wanted. Honesty was never the best policy. Telling the boss what he wanted to hear always worked. "I don't know, Skip." He had almost said 'Skipper,' but he didn't want to get lulled into a false sense of security, get familiar enough to use the name the employees used, but never in his presence.

"I don't believe it. Bunch of bullshit if you ask me. If a man's doing well, why punish him?"

"I agree."

"Yeah, well, I only bring it up because you've got the best record of any driver on our crew. You've got seniority, too. Every dog deserves a bone, and any dog as loyal as you deserves a shiny white milk bone."

Aaron leaned forward. He liked his dedicated route, hated change, but knew he couldn't protest. Refusing what Skip perceived as a gift would harm his reputation here, and hurt the man's feelings. "You come back," Skip said, "two days from now, and I'll have something special for you." He held up a hand to stay a protest that wasn't forthcoming. "You'll keep your dedicated route, but this is a one-off you'll enjoy."

"Okay." Aaron could live with that.

"I used to be a driver." Skip leaned back, stared at the corrugated tin ceiling of the hangar. "My best memory: I got to stay in a hotel in Seattle. I had a perfect view of the Space Needle. I had some downtime while they fixed my transmission. Got to see where both Bruce Lee and Jimi Hendrix were buried. Not bad, huh?"

Neither of those men were personal heroes of Aaron's, but he nodded nonetheless. "Yes sir." He winced on his own deference, but Skip didn't seem to mind the robotic loyalty. Blaincock slid a piece of paper over to Aaron, having basked sufficiently in his own benevolence. "Take a look at that."

Aaron picked up the paper. It was an application. "You see that shit? Coffee stains." He punched his finger against the surface of his metal desk and it echoed loudly. "Anyone who'd bring in application with coffee stains on it ain't getting hired here. Only one thing will put the kibosh on your employment opportunities at Nebraska Meats faster than a shoddy application. Know what that is?"

This one Aaron knew, from an orientation reel that was screened for him when he was a new employee. "A poorly-maintained POV."

"That's right." Skip beamed so brightly that Aaron got the temporary impression that he wanted to reward his employee with a literal bone to compliment the figurative one he would be handing out in a couple of days.

"If a man will put a dent in his own personally owned vehicle how do you think he is going to treat one of our trucks?"

Aaron waited long enough to establish whether or not the question was rhetorical, and Skip continued speaking a moment later, proving that it was. "You use your bobtail as your POV, right?"

"Yeah, I do." He noticed he called the Skipper neither "sir" nor "Skip" that time. His boss seemed to sense the omission too, but let it pass.

"I approve of it when employees use their rig as a personally-operated vehicle. It teaches you to care for the thing more, and—"

"Skip," Rhonda's voice came over an in-house intercom that was retrofitted from an old *Cobra* CB radio. "James Kiley just got violated for going over eighty hours in a seven day period."

"You see," Skip said, swiveling backwards to grab the handset for the two-way intercom. "You're Old Faithful, Neblett. The rest of these sons' a bitches need to be put out of their misery like Old Yeller."

Aaron stood, waited a moment. Skip Blaincock nodded and waved, letting Aaron know that it was okay to go. Before Aaron went, however, Skip held up his index and middle finger, and pointed them both at Aaron. He paused from speaking to Rhonda about Kiley's faux pas and mouthed the words "Two days," tapping the face of his watch in order to give his employee to understand that he was talking about increments of time. Aaron nodded, and got out of there.

He walked across the catwalk, down the metal stairs that always trembled uneasily as the cacophonic symphony of the place, its endless clang, shook everything metal to its foundation like a ceaselessly vibrating tuning fork.

Chapter Five

This stretch of Route 83 was undulating rock waves, stretching so far into the horizon it appeared that the bank of clouds over yonder was actually smoke rising from the ground, a mushrooming white explosion emerging from the fissures in the overgrazed tableland of North Platte, Nebraska. The view on either side of the road was as plain as the way ahead was beautiful. There were rusted grain elevators, fronted by cows resigned to their slaughterhouse fate, and a lonely road grader chugged along the right-hand shoulder.

Aaron turned left, down a road dotted with lodgepole pines, onto a stretch of back road that had slipped into irrelevance shortly after the Civil War, and was now the kind of place where one might find oneself stranded in the Witness Relocation Program. There was a stack of newspapers and coupon books collecting on his front porch, as well as several items of mail sprouting from his mailbox.

One of the first bits of advice he got as an over-the-road trucker was to either get a P.O. Box or to have a neighbor get his mail before it accumulated in a pile large enough to attract the unwanted attention of robbers casing the neighborhood. Aaron didn't care, though, partly because there were bars over the only two windows that would have granted access to his house, but mainly because anyone dumb enough to break into his home would quickly discover that Aaron Neblett could only be feared, not victimized.

He hopped down from the cab and went to the headache rack on the back of the truck. He opened the cab guard with the key he kept on a chain around his neck, reached into the Ziploc where it was nestled among the traffic cones and road flares, and he extracted one of the double-wrapped prophylactics. Holding it in his left hand, he relocked the box with his right, and stepped down. He then walked to his front door, unlocked it, and entered his house.

"Honey, I'm home."

There was of course no "Honey" to greet him, and Eros Erotic did not send their escorts this far into the sticks on outcalls. There was not even a dog to welcome him. The house was empty save for the basement, where he intended to go in a moment.

He walked into his small kitchen, took a frying pan down from a hook above the stove, and set it on the burner. He turned the gas on, poured a dram of Canola oil into the pan, and walked out onto his back porch, while the stovetop began to sizzle. On the back porch, there was a freezer with the bulky dimensions of a tanning bed, its smooth edges like those of a coffin. It hummed, a low Freon growling rumble.

Aaron Neblett opened the freezer and grabbed a sheet of Nebraska Meat bison patties, from where they were nestled next to the head of one of the many men he killed. Even with the thick layers of permafrost which accumulated over the months, it was clear that the head belonged to what was once a black man. The head was almond-shaped, and bore a crease down the middle of the crown. The bits of stubble and razor bumps on the face had hardened during the tenure of his perpetual winter inside the freezer. Aaron took his patties into the kitchen and began to cook them, flipping them with the spatula while he thought about how his path first intersected with that of the man who owned the head in his freezer.

Aaron had pulled into a lot, prepping for some sleeper berth time followed by a long, hot shower that would be free, thanks to the accumulated rewards points on his Frequent Fueler's card. He had been listening to useless CB chatter about the largest cutthroat trout someone had caught, and the most points on a buck they downed during deer season. This was interrupted by the approach of a lot lizard, a frizzy-haired woman in a red-sequined tube top wrapped underneath a denim jacket with a rhinestone pattern which glittered under the mercury vapor lamps.

Aaron whistled to get her attention, but she didn't seem to hear him, or was actively ignoring him. She went over to a liquid tanker with an egg-shaped "Danger/Cuidado" payload shining from the fluorescent glare of the Super America fuel canopy, where it was parked among several others in the teardrop-shaped lot.

He contemplated tugging his horn, but realized even in the depths of his horny lust that the horn was useless for doing anything but terrifying other people. He banged on the outside of his cab door with his left hand and stroked his erection with his right. He had a new vibrating egg that he wanted her to try on him, if only he could get her to come over here. He took his right hand off his hard-on to reach for the money clip he kept it in the cup holder between the seats. It was at that moment he spotted the man sneaking up on the left in his convex mirror, a woman's sheer stocking pulled over his face and compressing his nose flat into his low cheekbones.

Aaron played dumb, pretended to keep watching the lizard as she shimmied, her little pear-shaped ass writhing under her sequined bottom like a boa constrictor's muscles beneath an easily-shed layer of skin. The man jumped into the cab holding his sawed-off Mossberg in unsteady hands, and Aaron caught him with a roundhouse chicken-wing, an elbow to the Adam's apple that made the man forget all about the robbery in progress, and forced him to focus on more immediate concerns, like breathing, as his shotgun slid to the back of the cab.

The trucker quickly pushed the man through the curtains of his cab, back into the sleeper hold. He ripped his shower curtain from the standing-room only bathroom, placed it across the floor, and commenced with his grisly work. He started by dragging his antler-handled knife across an imaginary line he picked out just below the point on the Adam's apple where he bruised the stickup artist. He decided to keep the head, and discarded the body somewhere along Route Sixty near Socorro, New Mexico.

The burgers were done now, charred to perfection. He slid them out of the pan, turned the range off, and placed the patties on a plate. He was pretty sure the girl in the basement still had water, but he grabbed an artesian eight-ounce bottle from the refrigerator just in case. It was possible that she was on the other side of the door down there, waiting to clobber him with something, anything she managed to fashion into a weapon over the last few days that she was trapped here. The bolt lock on his side of the door showed no signs of strain, though, and there was not so much as a single errant paint chip on the floor.

Aaron Neblett pulled the bolt to the side and swung the door open, feeling vulnerable with his hands so full. "Hello?"

There was no reply. The available light in the room shifted from the left of the empty concrete expanse to the right, based on where the single bulb on a string decided to dangle. As the light swung, he saw her shadow, a long silhouette, the prone profile of someone who had given up. She was lying on the divan, the only piece of furniture in the room he provided her.

"Hello?" He tried again.

He saw the gallon jug of water next to her. It was half-empty, which was good. It meant she had decided to drink. Her body was motionless, and for a fleeting moment he feared that she might have found a way to kill herself, even with the precautions he took before setting out on the road.

"Hey," he said, leaning down to the ground. He slid the plate with two burgers across the floor. He also rolled the bottle of water across the concrete. "I have food, burgers, and drugs, too."

She rolled over. "Mm?" It was less a question than a protestation at the return to consciousness. It was deeper than crankiness. It was a sound that said she not only didn't want to be awake, but might resent being alive as well. But she finally spoke. "Drugs?"

"Drugs."

The girl sat up, rubbed her reddened cheeks with the open part of her pale palm. She suddenly scrunched up her face until her nose and frenulum nearly touched. Aaron watched her, perplexed. There was this odd lambent shift in her from one moment to the next. One second, she was a child, regressed and pouting. At the mention of drugs, she was suddenly jaded and as bitter as a widow or divorcee who had been on the wrong end of too many infidelities. She did not for a moment seem to be a creature who owned her own age, though. It was anyone's guess how old she was exactly, and Neblett had her pegged somewhere in the nebulous region between fourteen and twenty.

"What kind of drugs?" She said.

"I don't know," he said, pulling the condom out. "Jefe usually gave me bodies to transport, thirteen-hundred a head for migrant workers. Maids, construction workers."

"Huh?" Her squint returned, the perplexed expression of a child encountering cursive for the first time.

"Nothing," he said. "If you know something about it, maybe you can tell me."

He searched around for somewhere to pour the dope out, realized there were no mirrors and no plates (save for the one covered in bison and cooking grease). He dug his heavily-weighted keychain from his pocket, dipped a key into the condom, and brought it back out of the rubber a moment later, the silver grooves filled with a white powder covered in a yellowish scummy film. "Here," he said.

She leaned forward, straining to remain seated on the couch while also going in for the bump. It was some demented inversion of the airplane ritual that mothers used to trick their babies into eating applesauce. She tooted, a long snort that made her blink, caused her ginger red lashes to flutter. She gripped her tear ducts with one hand and pushed her nearly-white blond hair back from her scalp.

"Oh my god," she said.

"What?" Aaron asked, standing.

She stood too, and waved her hands in front of her face, fanning the fingers, fluttering them like someone who ate too much wasabi or was buckling under a four-alarm chili challenge. "Are you okay?" Aaron asked. He was afraid she was overdosing. He didn't want her dead.

"It's good. It's only been stepped on like, once."

"What does that mean? Stepped on?"

"It hasn't been cut much. Maybe a bit of baby formula and like some quinine. It's Peruvian flake."

She sat back down on the orange divan, and then lay prone, as straight, motionless, and limp as a slab of beef. She put her hands to her temples. "I can't feel my face."

Aaron held out the drooping condom to her, its bottom still weighted with the white sand. "Here, you can have the rest of this."

She opened her eyes. A bit of blood spilled from her nose. A reddish snot globule expanded, and then exploded on her face. "What do you want for it?" She asked, dreading the answer but accepting it before the reply came, agreeing to the bargain before she heard the terms.

She knotted the condom and slid it between the white mounds of her freckled breasts. "You want to fuck me?"

Aaron kneeled in front of her. "I don't want to fuck you." He reached for her face with a finger and attempted to wipe away a smudge of blood.

She turned her head with the speed at which a rattler coils. An errant bang fell from behind her ear, and became matted to the blood on her cheek. "Then what? You want to watch me fuck someone else?"

"What's your name?" He gave up on stemming the tide of red pouring from her nose. He stood up, and backed up a couple of feet, giving her the berth one might afford a Rembrandt roped off with red velvet.

"Luscious."

"Not that." He was more forceful, the worship dissipating from his tone now that he was standing and she was sitting. "Not the little lot lizard name you used when you hopped into my cab." He left out the part where he sapped her with his little mail-order beaver tail blackjack.

"Amy," she said, quietly. "Now, can you please tell me what you want for this?" She pointed to the slimy coke-filled condom nestled in her cleavage. "I would like you to give me my purse back, and I would like to make a couple of phone calls. Just let me keep this half ounce, and tell me what you want me to do for you."

"I don't want you to do anything for me."

"What do you want then?!" She banged her fists into the couch, found herself frustrated by the soft unresponsiveness of the cushions. She was forced to be satisfied with digging her nails into the lifelines of her palms, until her knuckles were white and the blood almost spilled from the translucent skin of her hands. "You want to watch me fuck someone else? Just tell me what you want."

"I want you to be my friend."

They were both quiet for a moment, stunned into silence and confusion. "I don't want to fuck you. I want you to come with me on the road for the next few days. I want you to massage my shoulders, say good morning." He paced, walked in circles, and came to stand underneath the only light in the room. He scratched the rough scrub of his beard. "I want someone to ask me how I am."

Amy's lips curled. She showed her teeth, or more properly bared them, as if something more noxious than a sulfur bilge just passed them by, or there was perhaps an errant fume from a paper mill borne on the breeze. "I wouldn't even know how to charge for that shit." She began rubbing her nose.

"I'll make it simple for you. I'll clean you up, and give you your phone back, provided you don't call the cops." He waited until she nodded before speaking again. "You can have your purse. I'll buy you some clothes. And if you stick with me for the next week or so, I'll keep you in coke. When we part ways, I'll give you whatever dope I have left. And I have a lot."

Amy nodded, repressing a sly smile, as a car dealer might when a potential customer walked on the lot and asked to pay sticker price on a sedan. "Yeah," she said. "That's cool."

"Okay. You ready to come upstairs?"

"Yeah."

They both stood, and climbed the basement stairs one at a time, up into the small kitchenette. No one had touched the burgers on the plate he brought downstairs.

Chapter Six

The Emporium was an ice cream parlor housed in a converted pharmacy, complete with vintage Rockwell-era Sealtest posters, featuring dimpled milkmen delivering glass bottles to rosy-cheeked housewives over waist-high fences. Behind the old apothecary were a petting zoo, and a miniature golf course that included eight kidney-shaped holes, each equipped with a colorful obstacle of some sort, ranging from a crocodile to a Bavarian windmill.

Aaron and Amy sat at what had once been a perfume counter, eating their desserts. Aaron was eating a large slice of apple pie, its flaky crust scorched to a crème brûlée consistency. Amy was eating the same, only topped with a globe of vanilla ice-cream. They sat without looking at each other.

"So..."Amy said, "how long will we be gone?"

Aaron set down his fork, and proceeded to eat what remained of his pie with his hands. "Three or four days, maybe a week tops. After that, I'll cut you loose. It's a promise."

She looked at him for a moment, and then went back to eating. She had eaten so little over the last few days that it was probably best to take it slow. She had initially planned to hit him over the head with something (or perhaps gouge an eye or testicle) when he finally came down the stairs into the basement, but after a determined sentry of countless hours waiting faithfully for her revenge, Amy Loeher gave up on getting even with the bastard who had locked her down there, at least for the short term. She had fallen asleep, and by the time she woke up, he was standing over her and it was then too late to try anything. He had done enough with that one half-ounce of coke to undue the week's worth of inconvenience he had put her through, and thoughts of harming him or trying to escape were now put out of mind. As long as he kept the baggies coming, he was entitled to his quirks.

Trying to finagle so much as an eight-ball out of her pimp, the GOD himself, was nearly impossible. He made her and Conchita and the rest of his girls keep receipts on all the purchases they made, and he expected reimbursement. She could use this weeklong break from him, she thought, downing the rest of her ice-cream in one gulp.

The kidnapping provided more than enough pretext for a week's absence or two. Tricks did weird shit like this, especially to young girls like her. When she finally got back to God, she would embellish the tale, add a story about a week in restraints in some dungeon to keep him from slapping her for being out of pocket and taking a vacation without his permission. She would make it sound good, as if she had barely escaped death at the hands of a homicidal maniac, which maybe she had. Amy would wait a couple of days to call God, even though the trick had already given her phone and purse back.

"You ready?" Aaron Neblett stood, scraping his chair against the floor. His eyes were inscrutable behind his red mirrored shades, a dull and sour expression covering the rest of his bearded face.

"Yeah." She stood with him.

He walked toward the back of the store. "Let's go look at the goats," he said.

She stopped halfway to the door, and he turned just before stepping outside. Amy was short, he noticed, only at eye level with the top row of the sunglasses and postcard carousels. "Get what you want. I'll pay for it."

Amy selected a pair of wraparound bug-eyed Oakley glasses, their lenses grossly oversized and resembling a Fokker aviator's mask, with the price tag dangling from the nose. She put them on. She adjusted to seeing the world through the reddish sepia tint of the glasses, and thumbed through the postcards on the adjacent carousel. She found one to her liking, and handed it to Aaron. He walked over to the cashier, an older hair band casualty who kept her coiffure sprayed as a figurative torch lit for a power ballad group that had broken up a long time ago, and was probably not getting back together again for a reunion tour.

The woman's hollow eyes rolled from Aaron to the girl. "This, and the glasses," Aaron said.

"Seventeen-fifty."

He handed the woman a twenty. "Keep it."

He walked outside, and Amy followed after him, the cashier's eyes following both of them. Outside, the sun was bright but mellow, a force more seen than felt, a soft yellow that made an alternating lattice of shadow and light as it broke through the trees shading the small ranchland. Several families walked to the edge of the old Amish worm fence, cautiously feeding handfuls of grain to the goats who worked their heads through the wooden staves to eat from the hands of giddy children.

"You've got to dump all the IDs you have, except one," Aaron said.

"Why?" She was looking off to the right, where a grandmotherly woman in a gingham apron worried caramel corn with two scoopers, moving it along a metal trough to a point where the corn was gathered in cellophane bags and wrapped by a younger girl, possibly her daughter.

"You want some?" Aaron asked.

Amy twitched bodily for a moment. It was the same involuntarily movement she made when he first gave her the bag of coke. Whenever he offered her something, he noticed, she performed a momentary calculus, wondering what it would cost her. He wanted something more than sex, she knew, something worse whose price might be too high for her, if she did not learn to say "no," and soon.

"Okay," she said.

She asked herself what exactly it was that he wanted. She waited in place under the shade of a tree, while he went over to the woman doling out the caramel corn. It wasn't love, she knew. She had met tricks who had wanted that, a fat-in-the-middle software programmer and one a bald ballistics engineer from the Navy, who was always working on PowerPoint presentations when she got called up into his hotel room. What then, she asked herself again, did he want?

Aaron paid the woman, tipped her, and gave Amy her bag of caramel corn, still hot. "If we get pulled over or something and the cops find a bunch of IDs on you, it'll look bad."

They walked back over to the fence. An insolent goat with an off-white beard and shofar-like horns approached them. "You got an ID that says you're eighteen?" Aaron asked.

Amy dug into her purse, a Vuitton knockoff. "Yeah." She rifled through the laminated cards. Aaron reached his hand into her purse, taking the cards from her. He went through them one at a time.

"This one won't work. No one will believe you're twenty-two." He sifted through a couple of more cards. "Here. Nineteen years old is a stretch, but believable."

He handed her the one card back, and kept the others. Amy held the card between her fingers. "Jenny Wentworth?"

"All right, Jenny. What's that?" He pointed at the postcard she held. Something like a smile appeared on his face. At least, he wanted it to be a smile, thought it amounted to a savage display of teeth.

"Oh," she said, handing it to him. "Here. You can have it."

He deflated, taking the card, realizing as he did that nothing could make her belong to him in the way he wanted, not the promise of drugs or the threat of violence. He wanted her to show him the card, explain the significance of it, why she selected it over the others. But she had stopped him cold. The single syllable, the distant ring of it, echoed in his head. "Here," it said, a short punch like the pneumatic *pop* of a single shot from his .38 Taurus.

There was no way to reach her, he knew. There was no way for him to reach anyone, to stretch across the expanse between the little bit that he was now and all that he had been, all that he had left behind, losing a bit more of himself with each life that he had taken. Some of the truckstops had little nondenominational chapels, ecumenical shelves cut from the unvarnished wood where a Catholic Mary was situated cattycorner to a very staid, unadorned Lutheran cross.

Aaron Neblett tried on multiple occasions to pray in the pews, asked for forgiveness from the void, not for the spectacle or the show of it (there was no one else besides him in the little chapels), but for a very real chance at salvation. It wasn't there, he decided, after about a minute of leaving deep impressions in the vinyl kneepads. So the killing would continue. Trying to slow a rig on a downward grade only led to brake fade.

The goat bleated, whining and moving toward Amy. She laughed a child's laugh, caught off-guard for a moment. Aaron tried not to give any indication that he was looking at her, lest she become self-conscious and hide what was so natural to her and such a rare sight for him. He watched her feed the goat caramel corn from the cellophane bag. He removed the mesh-webbed hat from his head and wiped his shoulder-length hair, slicking it back and then resituating the cap on his brow. He looked down at his feet in their steel-toed boots. Closing his eyes, he listened to the girl laugh as she fed the goats, and wondered if it wouldn't be prudent to perhaps kill her, or himself, or maybe both.

"Come on," he said, a moment later.

"What?"

"We've got to get on the road."

"Hold on."

Amy dropped the plastic bag on the goat's side of the fence, which began to snort the whole shebang, bag and corn, in two deep breaths. Amy ran to catch up with Aaron. "Are we heading out of town?"

"Yeah, but I can't say where, until I talk to the Skipper."

"Who's the Skipper?"

Aaron sighed deeply, giving her to understand that she should be quiet. She had been around men, especially the hitting kind, long enough to know what that kind of exasperation meant. God did the same thing, though his exhalations were usually followed up with a flurry of fists. They walked out to the truck in the front of the pharmacy/ice-cream parlor.

He was in the cab in less than three seconds. Amy, as both a newbie to the trucking game and a five-foot nothing female, struggled to get up. Aaron knew better than to hold his hand out to her, and he let her struggle. She pushed aside the plastic bag filled with dresses she had bought earlier today at Mode O'Day's, a fashion boutique downtown, and settled into her seat.

"Seatbelt," Aaron said.

She pulled the belt across her chest. Aaron turned the key in the ignition and allowed the diesel engine to wake up, as the various indicators and meters were roused to life. The Qualcomm, CB, and onboard computer were all awake now.

"It's like a spaceship," Amy said. She leaned forward, excited.

"You can adjust the weight on your seat," Aaron said, watching the mirrors that trembled from the horsepower of the engine as it made the reefer cab rumble. "It's on the right side of your seat."

He pulled out. "Why would you want to do that?" Amy said.

"Because," Aaron said, his rolling eyes hidden behind the tint of his shades, "it'll give you better shock absorption. Comes in handy on long trips."

"Oh. Can I get some cigarettes?"

"I'll buy you a pack, but no smoking in the rig, okay?" He was suddenly forceful. "You can set the cab on fire with one spark," he said, preempting the "why" that was coming.

"Okay."

"So, Jenny, are you my daughter or my niece, because you damn sure ain't my girlfriend."

"Niece," she said immediately, no doubt because it granted more distance, less relation.

"And what's your full name, in case someone asks you?"

"Jenny Wentworth." She dug through her phony Vuitton handbag and took some coke out, snorting a restaurant sweetener packet's worth of white dust from her fingerprints. She rubbed her fingers across her gums and closed her eyes to brace for the waves of brilliant light about to explode behind her eyes, the tinkling of something like glass going off in her synapses. A cacophony of church bells formed in her head, telling her that life was eternally exciting and she was beautiful.

"Can you roll my window down?" she asked. "Please."

Aaron hit a button in among the controls, and the wild Nebraskan crosswinds entered the cab. Amy leaned out, checked her reflection for bloody nostrils, and then watched the country blur like a green and blue whirligig unmoored from the axis of its pinwheel. Nebraska was ugly, plain, and flat, but for all of that it was peaceful, like the

Thorazine cocktail they gave her in Juvie. There was a diesel plant by the side of the road. The shifts were changing, and the pace of the workers who were punching in and punching out was virtually indistinguishable one from the other, because one group didn't want to be at work and there was truthfully not a lot for the other group to go home to.

There were soybeans, leafy rows rotated with blank furrows of red clayish dirt. They passed a closed and abandoned drive-in movie theater, where several children's seahorse toys had been ripped from their berths between the first row of drive-in seating and the blank white slate of the screen, the disused remnants of an old set of monkey bars weeping rust onto the sandpit below. Several red marquee letters were scattered across the ground.

Amy let her hand drift into the wind, allowing her flat, outstretched palm to be carried on a peaceful current that tossed her fingers as carelessly as a ragdoll or a paper airplane. Aaron snuck glances, afraid to speak. His hands sweated on the steering wheel. He was terrified of her naturalness.

"There's someone right behind you," Amy said.

"I know."

"So why don't you speed up?"

Aaron shook his head. "Rule number one. Never speed up in a rig when you're being tailgated. They'll just speed up, too, and stay behind you. Truck's slower than a four-wheeler.

Nothing can be done for it. If he doesn't like it," Aaron said, watching the little Volkswagen in his mirror, "Let the bastard pass me on the left."

She lost interest in the blurring scenery outside of the window. "Is there anything I can do?"

"Not right now." Aaron's stare remained fixed on the straight edge where the sky met the road on the horizon. He was in driving mode, not killing, philosophizing, praying, or talking mode. "Maybe later."

They drove through a small town, a little settlement with a True Value hardware store at its center and a little league diamond at its far edge, the kind of place old enough to have built all of its signs facing north in order to minimize the amount of damage the sun could do to the posted "Welcome" and "Pop. Size" signage. It was an inconsequential burg whose place beneath the overpass feeding into the loop of the highway gave the impression of being a lamprey on the belly of a massive, slowly drifting concrete whale, or a barnacle on Gibraltar Rock.

The Kenworth moved on a wide turn radius going into the Nebraska Meats compound. Aaron parked in next to an impressive Coronado semi that sat bobtail naked. He turned to Amy. "Stay here." He opened his door, readied to hop down, and remembered something else. "Oh, next time you do your little thing, please do it where I can't see you, okay?"

Amy nodded without looking at him, as if he were a parent making an idle threat. Aaron closed the door, hard enough to make her jump in her seat. She trembled and chewed the thumbnail on her left hand. Aaron walked up the main ramp, heading into the steel cathedral built to placate the pagan god of automotive industry.

He should really explain why it was necessary for her to sniff her coke out of sight, in a way that she would understand, he thought. If he was driving past a weigh station, and his E-Z pass blinked red rather than green, and he got pulled in for a Level III (the works) inspection, and the DOT cops went over his rig with a couple of K-9 units, then they were both heading to prison, his rig was getting impounded, and he could say goodbye to his CDL, all of his endorsements, his perfect driving record, and his patched jackets. He only had two of the three company coats left, now that one had been used to sop up blood down in El Paso.

"Old Faithful!" Skip Blaincock was on the catwalk, shouting and too excited to suppress his joy. "Come take a look, Aaron."

"Yes, sir."

Aaron scaled the steps two at a time, almost tripping and lunging face first into the windows of the Skipper's office. The pompadour was in slipshod shape today. A jellied strand had gotten loose and was now doing its own thing, as if Old Elvis had gotten carried away with his hound dogging gyrations and messed up his hair.

Skip held the door open for Aaron. "Did you see her?"

Aaron assumed he was talking about the Coronado out in the parking lot, and so he nodded. "Yes."

The rattling din of the place ceased the moment Skip closed the door. "You know how to get to Sacramento?"

"Pretty much a straight shot on Eighty until you hit around Provo or Salt Lake, and get a little curveball on Two-Fifteen. Then back on to Eighty."

"My man," Skip said, massaging Aaron's shoulders. "I knew there was a reason I tapped you for this job." He motioned for Aaron to sit down and took his own seat. "Look at this." Skip slid a black three-ringed binder across the table. There were page upon page of glossy printout images sleeved in Mylar. "Sacramento Sounds is unveiling their new tweeter and subwoofer combo pack. They need someone to drive their rig from trade show to trade show."

Aaron took the book in his hands while Skip continued selling it like a medicine show. "They're stopping everywhere: Nascar, auto shows, even..." Skip leaned in, larding it on in a conspiratorial hush-hush tone. "Even the Adult Video News Awards." He smiled and winked. Aaron suppressed the lurch in his stomach as his heart did a corresponding somersault or two, contemplating the array of she-cock, the hard-faced plastic surgery of the transsexuals, the steely androgyny of a not-quite woman who could put him in his place. Maybe even Chocolate Thunder would be there, if he kept the hammer down and made it in time.

He flipped through the images, and as he did, Skip provided a running commentary. “Guys who built the Budweiser Hydroplane designed the frigging thing. It’s a work of art is what it is.”

On one of the pages there was a schematic, a three dimensional diagram that showed the belly boxes beneath the tractor being deployed by an engineer seated at the AV console of the truck, toggling switches until the hydraulic system fully revealed an expanded showroom large enough to accommodate metal folding chairs, a visual display, and floorshow arrangements of high-end stereo equipment.

“It’s sweet, isn’t it?” Skip asked.

“Yeah,” Aaron said, thoroughly impressed.

“The cab’s a rock, man. She was used on a Springsteen tour. It’s got automatic, ten-speed everything. Your destination’s already programmed in there. You got three days to bobtail her there, a five day leg getting the word out about Sacramento Sounds, then back on home. Think you can handle it?”

Aaron slid the book back to his boss. “Sure.”

“Great,” Skip said, and smiled. “You’re going to California.”

Chapter Seven

The night clerk at the Extended Stay recommended The Nine Pin as a reasonable place to have lunch by day, and bowl at night.

Detective James Arklow sat with his back to a row of lockers used by league bowlers during competition, and he consumed two chili-cheese Coney Island wieners topped with thin drizzles of mustard. Maggie Loeher no doubt would not appreciate the liberal dose of chopped onions he was consuming, but if he could put up with the odor of cat piss and Virginia Slims in her house, she would just have to make due with his bad breath.

He scarfed both dogs quickly enough to know a bout of indigestion was only twenty to thirty minutes away. Fortunately, he managed to pay his tab and make it to the antacids in the glove compartment before his stomach could punish him for thinking he could get away with eating like a young man, when the truth was that he was coasting into his mid-fifties. His body, however, should have been grateful for small mercies. If he hadn't used his willpower to pass up on that piece of pumpkin pie, it would have required him to pump two units of insulin with his Eli Lily pen, just to get his blood sugar down to 200 again. If he kept at it with these diners (and the Extended Stay vending machines) it might, he told himself, eventually cost him a toe or two.

The weather was fair, the sun hidden, and the wind mild. He turned onto Boniface Drive, where an elderly woman pruned the berry bushes in front of her house. She waved to James as he passed, her hand unsteady and her arm roped with purplish varicose veins. He smiled and waved back, impressed and somehow heartened that she was able to do yard work this late in life. He pulled into Maggie Loeher's driveway and parked.

The cat appeared in the window, frozen like an Egyptian bas relief for a moment, and then it disappeared. Margaret Loeher opened the door before he had a chance to knock. She held the screen door open for him. "Hello, Sherlock fucking Holmes...."

"How do you do, Mrs. Loeher?"

She coughed and walked into the living room. "I made you some lemonade. Just in case you get thirsty while you're working."

He blanked, almost asked her what she was talking about, and then remembered. She studied him and the clothes he wore, a pinstriped Oxford shirt and red suspenders, Italian wingtips with fawn-colored spats. He liked to dress up when he was on a case, unless he was doing fieldwork rooting around in a creek bed or dumpster diving.

He rarely dressed up when he was teaching courses at Fairborn Technical College, partly because grading papers and coming up with a syllabus consumed so much of his time, but mainly because his students were usually so underdressed that if he were to attempt to appear professional, they would look at him as if he was from another planet. Besides, most of them were too busy texting or surfing the Web under the pretext of taking notes to even pay any attention to what he was saying, much less attenuate themselves to the effort he had put into getting dressed that morning.

"You ready?" Maggie asked.

"Sure," the detective said. He stuffed the end of his tie between two buttons of his Oxford shirt. Maggie Loeher put her cigarette out in an ashtray on the glass coffee table facing the television. Several lottery tickets, all losers, were on the table. Bits of metal shavings, and the penny that had been used to scrape the cards, were scattered across the glass.

On TV, there was a segment entitled "The Secret Life of the Fuhrer." Hitler and Eva Braun were frolicking in rare colorized home movies. "Do you think my daughter's still alive?" Maggie said.

The detective rolled up his sleeves. "If she is, I think someone has her."

"Why?"

"When people try to get lost, change identities, whatever, they're not very good at it, especially young kids." Detective Arklow made his way into the kitchen, carried the pitcher of lemonade and the glass into the backyard. Maggie Loeher followed him. "It's like this," the detective said. "Let's say Amy decided she wanted to start stripping again. And she was using another name. What name would she use? Probably something like Andrea Lerner, something similar to her old name. If she decided she wanted to go to school, maybe get certified as a phlebotomist or something, my guess is she wouldn't think twice about putting in a forwarding request for her mail, or maybe requesting old transcripts from her previous high-school. I'm not underrating her intelligence, just saying there are a lot of common mistakes people make when they're trying to disappear, and my guess is she would have made at least one of them by now, if she wasn't in some kind of trouble."

The detective stopped speaking, focused now on the lawnmower before him. It was a rusted manual push mower, a green and yellow John Deere deal that reminded him of the old *Fisher Price* popcorn push toys that he used to keep his nephew busy from time to time. He had never told his sister about his condition, but she had seemed to intuitively sense that he wished he had a child, and she had let him watch her son on occasions.

"So what do you think happened to her?" Maggie picked the pitcher and lemonade up from the lawn chair where James had set them a moment before. She poured herself a glass and drank it down.

The detective removed his holstered air-weight .38 from his belt and set it on the wooden bannister of the back porch's staircase. He hesitated for a beat. He did not want to give it to her straight, but she had asked. "She's either been abducted, or she's dead." He studied Maggie's face to see how she would take it.

She took it, because she had no choice in the matter. "If she's dead…."James assumed she would trail off at that point, unable to contemplate the idea. But she spoke again, a moment later. "If she's dead, I'll kill myself."

"I won't let you do that, but right now, we have to find out where she is, or what happened to her. I know this sounds awful, but knowing she's dead is better than not knowing what happened to her."

"Closure," Maggie said, putting grim air quotes around the word, her mouth twisted perhaps by the bitterness of the lemonade, or more likely contorted by the cliché of the concept. "I go to this group for people whose loved ones have disappeared. That's what they call it. Closure."

"Right," James said, moving the mower to the far edge of the lawn. "But we'll cross that bridge when we come to it."

Maggie poured another glass of lemonade. "We'll fuck that chicken when we catch it."

She left this glass on the unfinished wooden rail of the back porch. "Lemonade's there when you want it," she said, and walked back inside of her small house. She sat down on the glider chair with the cat lounging across its back, its front two paws resting above its master's breasts. She reached among the already-scratched lottery tickets for her cigarettes, lit one and watched Hitler as he spoke to Arno Breker and Albert Speer in front of the Eifel Tower.

James had mowed two rows of grass already, the difference probably visible from a crop duster, a couple of short alleys of AstroTurf to his left and calf-deep elephant grass on his right. The sun appeared from between the clouds, as if it knew that he was going to do manual labor and thought now would prove the best time to beat against his back with its heavy, stinging rays. He cursed and mowed, audibly pissed because that was the de facto mood a man was supposed to be in whenever a woman tricked him into doing anything around the house it had not been his initial intention to do. A man would re-shingle a roof in July without complaint, provided it was on his list of preplanned chores. But running so much as a snake down the toilet at another's behest was somehow galling for him. He had lived alone in his apartment for years, and it had been a long time since he had done anything like this.

Beneath the mild frustration, though, he was grateful for the activity. The labor of it was good for firing up the mind. No diesel, no electricity, just elbow grease and blades of grass flying against starched khakis and Italian leather, pools of fetid wet sweat forming underneath the armpits of his white shirt, and a drooping wet Pangaea shape appearing in the small of his back and dripping downward. He asked himself what the next move would be, how best to proceed on the case. The flying blades of grass made his eyes sting and his lips chap.

He called his notepad to mind, trying to remember what was written there without taking a glance, without having to reach into his back pocket. Step one, he remembered, was to ask about the father. If he was still alive and in the picture, then he was a suspect. If there had been any custody beef, his name would get a little circle and asterisk.

He pushed the mower, the yard half plumb, shaved as cleanly as the head of a recruit fresh from a basic training barber's chair. The idea that Amy Loeher was running around homeless was not plausible. Shelters had rules that anyone living there had to abide by, and if Amy had been a big enough handful to get caught in the Juvenile Justice system more than once, it was a lock that she wouldn't be able to put up with the terms they would impose on her at the missions.

If she was a drug addict and she had been stripping, then it was a safe bet that she had eventually graduated to tricking, in which case she had either been abducted, murdered, or was still selling herself, probably under an assumed name and under the supervision of a pimp. She may have been doing as much when she was still living with her mother, and Maggie was either too blindly naïve or ashamed to admit it to the detective today.

James was winded and hot now, and the four-in-hand knot of his tie which slowly wrapped itself around his neck did not help matters much. He undid the top two buttons of his Oxford shirt, and felt the beginning of blisters form on his hands as he removed his paws from their heated grip on the push mower. The cold glass of lemonade felt good on the padded insides of his hands, the icy condensation dulling the throbbing pain which had been worsening as he gripped the lawnmower tighter and tighter, using all of his strength without realizing it, his mind on the case while his body, unbeknownst to him, had almost mown the whole lawn.

There were only two furrows of high grass to go before he could successfully declare to Maggie Loeher that he had undone probably a year's worth of neglect. He stared out over his handiwork, and realized as he gazed on the remaining rows that he would have to exercise caution when mowing near the graves of Mr. and Mrs. Butterworth. The weeds would remain high around the little white crosses of the gerbils, a bit of respect paid to the miniature cemetery in the far right corner of the lawn. James doffed his glass of lemonade to the little dead rodents, and drank.

He finished the glass, set it down, and fought off the nagging sensation, the creep of an idea that almost made him laugh at its preposterousness, but which he knew he would now have to pursue. A hunch was its own form of torture, an irrational instinct, a beckoning that had nothing to do with training, or with what he told his students in class, but everything to do with being a detective. He turned around, watched Maggie as she worked a little Isoflex stress ball in her hands while watching the boob tube.

The detective chewed the ice cubes in his mouth and walked back inside, basking in the cool AC that pressed his shirt against his front and back, dried the sweat against his armpits until he itched uncomfortably. "Mrs. Loeher."

"I'm getting ready to hit the keyboard," she said, running the little latex ball in her hands, passing it from finger to finger and then holding her hands in a prayerful Karate chop motion, keeping the ball suspended in both hands as she squeezed her grip around it from either side. "Got to warm up."

"Did you bury the hamsters in the backyard?"

"Gerbils," she said.

"Did you bury them?"

"Amy did. Why?"

"Did you watch her bury them?"

Mrs. Loeher ceased moving the little saline-filled ball in her hands. "No." She almost asked "Why," but stopped herself short. She knew why he asked. The disbelief that had been his burden a moment before was now hers. "No," she said, laughing. "No way...."

"Probably not, but maybe. There are probably two dead hamsters in those boxes-"

"Gerbils."

"Rats," James said, holding his hands up. He rarely lost his cool, especially not with students or clients. But he was hot and tired, and did not want to cut the lawn anymore. "Do you have a little shovel?"

"There should be a little garden spade outside there," Mrs. Loeher said, pointing toward the backyard.

"Right." He walked back out into the heat of the day. He looked down and noticed that the cuffs of his slacks were a deep fungal green. "Shit." He searched along the perimeter of the wooden staircase of the crumbling patio, looked at the ground, spotted a little metal trowel, rusted of course, leaning against a wooden fence post. "Gotcha." He walked over to pick it up.

Maggie Loeher stood up, dropped her little stress ball, and forewent the rest of her diet of television for the day.

James leaned down and stabbed the earth in front of the rodents' graves. He worked the husband's plot first, removing a three-by-six inch plot of grass and dirt in one shovel, working the remaining clods of mud away from the little shoebox casket until he could pull it free of the ground with both hands. Dirt slid underneath his fingernails, but he paid it no mind.

The little box smelled like one would expect a dead hamster to smell after six months of rotting. "What's in the box?" Mrs. Loeher asked.

James turned his head to the right, breathed deeply once, and pulled the cardboard top off the Footlocker box. A tiny skeleton, covered with molting tufts of brown hair, was curled into a fetal ball. As ugly and inconsequential as the thing was, Detective James Arklow felt a momentary pang for the rat, frozen in the eternal rictus of sorrow familiar in the faces of mummies and the prostrate victims of Pompeii.

He set the thing back in its box, replaced the lid, and lowered it back into the ground. Then he hastily covered it over with dirt. "God," he said, and spit a wad of saliva to his right side.

Maggie Loeher laughed behind him. He was happy she found him amusing. "I thought you've been around dead bodies."

"Dead bodies don't smell that bad." He began desecrating mama gerbil's eternal resting place.

He spaded the ground, preparing for the anticlimax, remembering how it looked when Geraldo Rivera had opened Al Capone's empty vault. This wouldn't be that embarrassing, though. That was live national TV, while his was an audience of one.

It was best to remain optimistic, and a little philosophical. If the Missus was in there, and not a note or a diary or something to that effect, he could cradle the small mammal's skull in his hands, strike a profile, and recite Hamlet's soliloquy, practice his dramatic skills so the day wouldn't be a total waste. "To be or not to be," he said, prematurely. "Tis nobler to something...something...."

He trailed off. He was in Criminal Justice, not the English department. This box was different, smaller and white. James opened it. There was a camera inside, its gunmetal coat scratched and broken in places. He blew the dirt away from the face of the camera and the USB port. He looked at Maggie Loeher.

"Where's Mrs. Butterworth?" She said.

"Do you have the USB cable that goes with this?"

She looked at him. It was clear that her understanding of technology extended to desktop Mahjong and email. "I'll check," he said. He grabbed his air-weight revolver from the bannister, clipped it back onto his belt, and walked back into the house.

"What are you doing?"

"Just trying to figure something out, Mrs. Loeher..." He knew not to bother looking upstairs. Whatever was worthwhile up there was now wasting away in cardboard boxes marked "Evidence" down at the station, where the lead detectives were probably presently engaged in arguments over the relative merits of chocolate-frosted versus glazed donuts.

James walked over to the computer and looked on the back. There was a compatible cord, linked to a little MP3 player, which most likely had belonged to Amy, and was exactly where she had left it charging before her disappearance. He disconnected the cord from the MP3 player without asking.

Maggie Loeher's knees popped with crepitus creaks as she kneeled down to grab a Virginia Slim from the table. James held up the camera, now attached to the USB cord, to Mrs. Loeher. "Do you mind if I take this back to my hotel room?"

She shook her head. "I don't mind." She picked the pack of cigarettes up from the table and shook it until a butt came loose, protruding from the pack. "You want one?"

He took one. "Thank you. I'll be back. Or I'll call you when I find something out." He put the cigarette in his mouth, realized he didn't have a lighter, and that his room at the Extended Stay was zoned as 'non-smoking'. It had been so long since he last smoked in earnest that he wasn't even sure if they still made 'smoking' hotel rooms. He leaned in and she lit his cigarette for him. He squinted, the butane making his eyebrow hot as the flame danced upward.

"Good luck," she said.

"Yeah." He took two puffs, winked, and walked out the front door. Two kids with squirt guns pumped rapid bursts of water at each other on the sidewalk, running around his car in circles as they shot at each other. He unlocked his door and got in, flashed his high-beams, and honked once to scare the kids away.

He cracked the sun roof to let the smoke out and ashed into the remains of his takeout Diet Coke from The Nine Pin diner. The sun had retreated across the sky, throwing weak rays that tinged the clouds with cotton candy pink edges. He smoked until the filter burnt his finger. He ditched the cigarette butt into the Styrofoam cup, and realized that he had forgotten to cut the last two rows of Maggie's lawn, where the garden gnomes still hid.

Chapter Eight

It was an exurb of undistinguished buildings, a flatland of prefab and identikit car dealerships and motels that covered the ground thickly, much like any of the bland, anonymous and interchangeable settlements which sprouted up around highways all across America. Driving through them and staying for a few days was a tolerable enough task. Trying to imagine what it would be to live there was an unbearable task for the detective.

The Extended Stay was nestled in a cruciform basin whose parking lot pressed flush against a sound barrier joined to a low retaining wall that did nothing to mitigate either the whooshing sound of cars tearing along the highway, or the sight of them as they drove beneath an overpass recently renamed for a soldier killed in Iraq.

James grabbed the camera off the passenger seat and got out of the car, locked it and walked to the side entrance of the hotel. He headed across the hall, the thin carpet soaked with the smell of chlorine tracked from the indoor pool. He opened his hotel room and walked inside, comforted by the dark transience of it. The Weather Channel was running on the muted television housed in a harvest gold cabinet. Thin bars of light snuck through the edges of the window's curtain, making patterns across the unmade bed. His laptop was on, the default screensaver some sort of amorphous blob that bounced from one corner of the screen to the other whenever he left it alone for more than ten minutes.

He turned on the bedside lamp, which sat on an end table where years ago there would have been a Gideon Bible, but now there was only a phone book and a complimentary mint. He grazed the cursor on his laptop and brought up a couple of internet windows, hoping that the intermittent connection he had sustained last night while checking his mail and browsing for pornography was now in a good mood.

In one window, the *Private Investigator Monthly Online* webpage was displayed, the twin symbols of a magnifying glass and a Holmes-esque deerstalker hat framing the image of this month's glossy cover of PIMO. Detective Arklow had been submitting articles to them for three years, and had received nothing but form rejections in that period of time. His most recent article, "Campus Civility" was an editorial dealing with how investigators should respect the rights of students and faculty when their cases took them into the college environment. He was not holding out much hope of an acceptance letter. He was, in fact, banking on another rejection via snail mail, which would be waiting for him in the faculty mailbox when he got back to Fairborn.

In another window, his homepage appeared, with an insert photo of himself and his CV prominently displayed. He brought up one of several bookmarks he used to aid him in his cases. *Tineye* was on his list just beneath *Reverse Lookup.* A small camera icon was on the right side of a search field where a cursor blinked, waiting for him to type something. He hooked the camera up to one of three USB ports on his laptop. He clicked the camera icon, and waited for his computer to finish its install. A new folder appeared, marked "Me and C."

James clicked on it. Three images showed up. The first was of Amy Loeher. She was wearing a pink rayon half-slip and she was spread across a bed. She pouted her glossy lips, and threw up a peace sign with her right hand. The next image, labeled "C.jpeg," was of a young girl, probably Hispanic (possibly Middle-Eastern) and about fifteen, he guessed. She wore a camouflage hoodie sweatshirt, unzipped far enough to display cleavage swelling out of the top. Most of her breasts were exposed, but she covered the nipples with her hands. The third image, "A-C" featured both Amy and the girl of undetermined ethnicity. It was a self-shot pic with both of them blurred slightly from the starry burst of an unmuted flash going off in a bathroom mirror. They were naked except for towels around their waists, as they stood back to back.

Returning to the *Tineye* window, he selected the first image and hit "Enter". He waited, the engine searching through millions of files, crawling across the entire span of the internet. He got only one returned search, and he clicked on it.

"Erotic Reviews" the page said. There was an entry with one of five possible stars filled with gold next to her image, and a review placed by "TheDonofthishit," an obvious net handle for someone who used a self-shot image of his own abdominal muscles photographed with a cellphone camera in some Gold's Gym wall-length mirror:

"This bitch isn't down for pretty much anything cept a straight fuck. Head w/ a condom. Stay away fellas."

It wasn't much help. James moved on to the second image, deleting the first and clicking on "C.jpeg." There was the same wait, the same load cycle that kept him in suspense as he prayed that he got some kind of hit. "0 Search results returned out of 1.23 billion images." He sighed.

There was a knock at the door. He jumped up, almost shoving the laptop off the bed, and nearly banging the back of his head against the wall as he went for the door. He looked through the keyhole, and saw through the fisheye refraction that it was a maid, with her cart by her side and a spray bottle in her gloved hand.

"No thank you," James said, putting his face against the door. "Please come back later."

"Okay. Sorry." She wheeled her cart away from the door.

James walked back over to the bed. He lay down, moved the cursor over the third image, "A-C.jpeg," and he put the *Tineye* to work. He waited. "1 Search results returned out of 1.23 billion images."

He clicked the one image that had been returned. "Nitekitten" was the name of the site, and the image was attached to an ad that had run for a week more than a year and a half ago, fortuitously cached until now. "Lushes N Cee," it said, in a distracting pink font that sparkled. The details of the advertisement were listed in the truncated and acronym-laden type that was so native to texting teenagers, and so alien to everyone else, especially to aging detectives.

"Double ur pleasure and double your fun. 2 girlz 4 da price of 1." A telephone number was listed below the picture which Amy had taken in the bathroom, and which had led James to this site. Below that, their terms were listed:

OUTCALL ONLY-150 roses for an hour-Sensual massage-prostate massage 300 roses an hour- ROSES ARE FOR TIME ONLY NO SEXX-DO NOT CALL FROM BLOCKED NUMBER OR USE FOUL LANGUAGE. RUDE MEN WHO DID NOT KNOW HOW 2 TALK TO GIRLZ WILL BE DISCONNETCED!

"Lushes," he said out loud, rereading it several times from the beginning. It was a teenage girl's phonetic approximation of the word "Luscious," the same name her mom said she had used when she was stripping at Bare Sensations. He thought back over what Maggie had said, about how her daughter had aced the Math and Science portions of the GED, but had come up snake eyes on the essay portion of the test.

Pain nested in his stomach, a strange but familiar agony that usually accompanied an especially cruel crime scene, which this website may have been in some abstract way, since at least Amy (and probably both girls) had been underage at the time the advertisement had been posted. Something about her struggling to spell "Luscious," and coming up with "Lushes" made his heart sting, the sexual precociousness juxtaposed with her naivety in probably almost every other area, including her ability to spell. He shook his head, tasted the sour remnants of the Virginia Slim he regretted smoking now.

He inhaled a deep breath and took out his cellphone, and the detective dialed the number that was listed on Nitekitten. It rang once, twice, and then someone picked up. "Hello?"

It was an older woman, someone's mother, James Arklow deduced. "Hi, I'm looking for Cee?" He tried the name out tentatively. If Amy had been going by Luscious (or "Lushes"), then the other girl was probably still using her working girl's handle as well.

"Cee?" The woman said. A baby cried in the background on her end, and she said something soothing to the infant in Spanish. "I guess you mean 'Conchita?'"

"Yes."

"Well, I got news for you, Gabacho. I have caller ID, and picking up underage girls is a felony. Not only that, but the police got a website where they put all your mug shots when they catch your ass, so your wife and neighbors can see what a piece of shit you are."

"Ma'am...." James took the phone away from his ear, let her rattle off for another thirty seconds or so. "Madam, I'm a detective. I'm not a John."

"Detective?"

"Yes ma'am. I'm working a disappearance."

"Yeah, but my daughter ain't disappeared. She's in 'Breaking Out' right now."

"Breaking Out?" James kept the phone pinned between his shoulder and chin, used his other hand to bring the notepad and pencil from his pocket. "Conchita is in 'Breaking Out?' " He said, repeating it, urging her to continue.

"Yes. What do you need Conchita for?" The baby was now silent on her end, perhaps feeding off her mood and ceasing to cry once she mellowed.

"Ma'am—"

"Don't keep calling me ma'am. You make me feel like you're a bill collector or something."

"Okay. Tell me your name then."

"Esmeralda," she said. "Orozco."

"Esmeralda, my name is James Arklow and I'm a detective. I need to know where your daughter, Conchita, is. She's fine, but I think one of her friends might be in real trouble."

"Breaking Out!" She shouted. "We already been through that."

"Right, where is 'Breaking Out?' " He didn't ask what it was, as he could probably guess.

"It's on Beaumont, downtown. It's in a big building all by itself, across from the library and the courthouse."

"Okay," James said, writing vigorously on the pad. "Thank you, Esmeralda."

"De nada." she slammed the phone down.

James closed the phone and rolled over. A woman spoke quietly about precipitation and gathering storm fronts on the eastern seaboard. A moment later she was shouting loud enough for the people in the adjoining rooms to hear the meteorologist give her weather report, before James finally found the control he had rolled onto and turned the volume on the TV down.

He was hungry, but this was shaping up to be a vending machine night, and he certainly needed a shower, could in fact smell his own ripeness, but more than either food or a shower he needed to know what Conchita knew. He threw a blazer over his Oxford shirt, with the sole purpose of concealing the air-weight pistol, and he headed out.

The sun was setting, forming a bleary red cover that turned an ugly orange when it met the waves of smog rising from the city below. James edged along with the traffic, slinking forward until he wended his way down into the valley and onto Main Street. He checked the clock on the dash, 6:18 p.m.

"Breaking Out" sounded like an inpatient residential drug treatment program, which meant she probably wasn't going anywhere soon, but if the desk nurse or whoever wasn't impressed by his bona fides and it wasn't normal visiting hours, his questions would have to wait until the morning.

The sidewalks were thick with corporate drones, all manner of legal and judicial suckerfish with leather attaché cases and khaki trench coats flowing in the wind as they rushed toward taxis and their cars scattered across the city, or in the bowels of underground parking garages. James wondered if at some point he would be called on to testify in this case, and he shook off the thought in the next moment. Taking the stand was only slightly less aggravating than a jury summons.

He saw the library on his left as he drove past, its facade a massive gothic picture of cornices and faux ionic columns. Surface parking wasn't happening, and with a city Metro bus bearing down on his fender, Detective James Arklow pulled into a pay lot manned by an African man who wore a white cloth turban. The man watched an old Schwarzenegger movie with Arabic subtitles on a portable television no larger than a lunchbox. He tore off a ticket and handed it to James, who parked facing a building where the bricolage of several fading advertisements blended together on the side of a pigeon-swarmed brownstone.

A whipping wind scattered fast food wrappers and sections of the local newspaper across the wet street. James crossed against the light, and ran up the block. He kept his cold hands in his pockets, and trotted until he was directly across the street from the library, that gray fortress where homeless men filtered in for warmth and the local high-school students went to work on their projects. He looked to his left, and heaved a sigh of relief. Mama Esmeralda may have been initially unhappy to hear from him, and she may have been distracted by the baby crying in the background, but she had steered him true.

"Breaking Out" was in a late Victorian-era house, probably endowed by the trust of some rich philanthropist, set back from the noise and the light of the city by a quarter-acre vegetable garden shielded by acorn trees, whose fallen shells littered the sidewalk on the path up to the front door. James walked up the steps and tried the door.

It was locked. He looked around. There, to the left, was a cobweb-covered buzzer nestled into the face of the building. He hit the button. There was a buzz, then a scratching noise.

"Hello?"

"Madam, my name is Detective James Arklow. I have reason to believe that one of the girls staying here might have information, which could lead to the resolution of a missing person case."

"We have no girls here," the voice snapped. "We only have young ladies."

"Ma'am, if you don't mind, I would like to speak to one of those young ladies."

He didn't want to get into a semantic tussle with the woman. If he hadn't needed her, the options would have been more varied, and his answer could have been far more colorful. "Who would you like to speak to?" The little speaker box asked him.

"I need to speak to Conchita. She may be able to help me find the young lady who is missing and may be in great danger."

That got her. The missing person was no longer sexless, potentially even someone perfidious enough to have a penis. It was a female, and he had relayed the information to her using the nomenclature she preferred.

"Okay."

The buzzer buzzed, and the wooden door vibrated. He grabbed the brass handle, half-expecting to get shocked, and opened it. The entryway was carpeted, the main room separated from the rest of the house by two doors which were both closed, leaving him to stand alone next to a coatrack. On the wall to his left, there was a black-and-white glossy poster of a young woman cradling her knees to her chest: "Pregnant and don't know where to turn?" There was a hotline number listed below.

On the other wall was a corkboard covered with various message pinned there with thumbtacks. There was a duty roster that listed which girls had which chores on an assigned day, and below that was a list of rules: "Absolutely no makeup-No earrings-no nail polish-no jewelry."

One of the two doors in front of him opened, and a woman with a horseshoe-shaped titanium nose ring entered the room. James pegged her as a staff member, since she was flouting the rules about 'earrings,' unless of course nose rings didn't count. She cleared up the confusion, held the door behind her open, and without taking her eyes off of him said, "No visitors are allowed after six at night. And no men besides counselors and maintenance workers are allowed onto the premises of 'Breaking Out' at any time."

A girl entered the room from the door the woman held open. James recognized her as a slightly more vibrant version of the girl from the picture he'd found on Amy's camera.

"But," the woman said, "This is an exception I'm willing to allow. If Conchita was uncomfortable with it, I wouldn't let her go through with this. But since she gave it her blessing, I'm going to let you talk to her in the activity room."

The woman, whose nametag above her left breast said "Jill," opened the other door with a key from the set she kept on a chain attached to her belt. She pushed the door inward and let James and Conchita enter.

"Thank you."

"Cee, are you comfortable talking to this detective alone, or would you like me to stay here?"

"You can go," the girl said softly, staring at her nonstick slippers.

James nodded to Jill, and she suppressed the dirty look she intended for him.

"Okay," James said. "Do you want to have a seat?"

He held out his hand toward a table welded to the floor and surrounded with plastic chairs. Conchita shuffled across the floor in her booties, as if ice skating, and pulled out a chair. "You got a cigarette?"

"Sorry," James said, and sat down a couple of chairs away from her.

"Fuck," she said, drawing the syllable out. She spoke slowly, with an accent in which her vowels were drawled. She had the speech pattern of what had been called a "Surena" for decades, until the word for Mexico's southern farmers was appropriated by gangs in the late 1980s, when he was still a cop on the Force. He guessed she spoke Spanish and English indifferently. There was about her an indistinct roughness, most evident in the residue of Dior-drawn eyebrows she wore that he had seen on SoCal girls who assimilated to the barrio subculture rather than to the middle-class lifestyle their parents had wanted for them.

"Do you know why I'm here?" James asked. The ice had to be broken, and he didn't want to come right out of the figurative gate with *Hey, so I saw your picture on the internet.*

"Yeah, you want to know about the boy I dated from Sinaloa, the one they say shot at the Border Patrol puto?"

"No, I'm not here to ask about anything that could implicate you or get you in some kind of trouble."

"Then what?" She twinned her fingers around each other, perhaps still thinking about that cigarette. She laughed, the oddly becoming gap between her teeth the kind of flaw that heightened beauty rather than lessened it. "When my girl Jill saw you at the door, she thought you were here for John School and you was lost."

He seemed to vaguely recall her mom mentioning something about Johns, but didn't think it necessary to mention it to Conchita. Any mention of having talked with her mother would have made her think his loyalties were divided. No detective ever got a teenager on his side by mentioning their parents.

"John School is I guess a diversionary program or something?"

"Yup, for guys who got busted and go to school and learn what their habits support. See?" She shoved a book at him, a plastic-covered three-ringed binder that sat on the table. The cover said "Death Book."

"I'm guessing there aren't prom photos in here," he said, opening the pages.

"Most of those girls was too young to go to prom."

Inside there were Polaroid images of girls who were unconscious or dead, garroted with extension cords, heads cleaved with hammers that matted their hair into painted sheets of red blood. "That's what the street will get you. It's not for me."

He continued turning the pages. One girl sat in a claw-footed tub, her wrists slit and the redness of the water diluted by a tap which had been left on and untended. "Once I complete my evaluation period this time, I'm going to get a job on staff here."

"That's good. This is not for you," he said, tapping the book. "Or anyone." He slid the book away from himself, sending it halfway across the table.

"Okay," she said, relaxing and leaning back in her chair. "Tell me what you want to know."

His seeming lack of interest had loosened her up. It was a technique that sometimes worked better with younger interviewees. "Amy Loeher. Do you know where she is?"

Conchita jittered her legs beneath the table and shook her head. "No. I wish I did."

"Do you know why she disappeared?"

Her soft eyes latched onto his. Something in her melted. She wasn't going to cry, but he could sense the effort she was making to keep her tear ducts clear. Whatever else she was, or had been, and whoever her former associations, it was obvious to James that she had actually been Amy's good friend. It was possible that she was the only one besides Maggie and him who cared about the missing girl.

"No. If I had to guess, that worthless nigga who had her tricking probably put her in a situation she couldn't get herself out of."

The door behind them rattled. James turned from his interview. Through the space in the door jamb he could see a shadow which no doubt belonged to Jill the counselor. "What worthless man?" James asked, knowing in the rough world she hailed from that "nigga" and "person" were virtually interchangeable. He once heard a stickup kid describe the delivery driver he had robbed as "a Chinese nigga."

Conchita sneered, would have probably spit if they had been outside. "God Body Divine," she said, shaking her head. There was disgust in her words, but also reverence, that foggy area where abuse and love became one for a certain type of woman, who thereafter could never separate them again, and became easily bored with men who failed to understand that much about them.

"God Body Divine. That's quite a title."

"He's a Five-Percenter. You know what that is?"

"I do."

In his endless research of extremist groups, from those responsible for the Achille Lauro bombing to Baader Meinhof, he had come across various fringe organizations both in his research and in his fieldwork. He had discovered white men who worshipped Odin, dreamed of bombing the pentagon, and hanging those who took part in miscegenation, as well as black men who believed that the white race had been created by a mad scientist hell-bent on causing suffering to the original man, aka the black man. “They're kind of like the Nation of Islam on steroids,” James said.

“Right.”

“Do you know where he is?”

“Yeah...” Her voice was soft, almost a whisper.

James leaned forward. “If you're worried about your safety, I can—”

The sneer returned. “I'm not scared of that nigga. He's scared of me. Shit, you think he wants it getting out that he was pimping us when we were fifteen? They'll lock his ass under the jail.” It was the first time she acknowledged that she had been a prostitute for God, and with Amy.

“Where is he?”

“He runs Kroc Houses. It's his apartment building.”

“He's a landlord?”

“He's a slimy, reptile-ass nigga, but I have to give it to him. He's slick.”

“How so?”

“He's slick enough to have had a mama-daughter team both hoeing for him without either one knowing about the other one.”

“And where do his girls stay?” James took out his pad and pencil stub.

"That's just it," she said, getting frustrated for the first time since their interview began. "Ain't you hearing me? He has the girls up in the apartments. When they hand him the money from their tricks, he puts it on the books as rent. He's even got a couple of real renters in there to make it look good."

"Do you know the address?"

"Here," she said, holding out her hands. James slid the pad and pencil across the table. She wrote on a blank sheet. "It's only like ten minutes from here."

"What does he look like?"

"A fat motherfucker." She laughed. "Like an ex-linebacker. He ain't too flashy. He's got dreadlocks. He wears those ugly Cosby sweaters."

"Coogi?" James said.

"Yeah. I'll never understand how something so expensive can be so ugly." She slid the pad back to James. He studied it, relieved to find that her handwriting was blocky and perfect.

"Does he carry a gun?"

"No. He's scared of getting locked up, and the only people he beats on are girls. But he does keep some guns in his apartment."

"Did he beat you?"

Conchita interlocked her fingers, took a deep breath and stretched her hands toward the ceiling, her diaphragm rising and sagging underneath her gray sweatshirt. "Yeah," she said, yawning quickly and then recovering. "But not like he beat Amy. He liked to beat on his white hoes. He said it was a black God's revenge on a white devil for slavery."

"How bad did he beat her?" He usually let criminals tangential to his investigation slide, but this guy was shaping up to be bad enough to warrant some attention.

"Sh-" She rolled her eyes, as if her words couldn't do it justice. "The worst was when he took a frozen chicken out the fridge and beat her with it till she lost control of her bladder. She was on the bathroom floor peeing for like two days."

James unwittingly picked his pencil stub up from the table, and jabbed the graphite end into his hand, almost breaking the point of his pencil and the skin of his palm. Conchita continued. "I also seen him take a...um...." She struggled for the right word, separated her hands far enough away from each other to show the dimensions of something imaginary, as if she was describing a fish she had caught. "It was like a dagger in its case?"

She looked at James. He nodded, and she resumed. "It was a dagger, and he kept it in the case, but he shoved it in her pussy until the handle—"

"Hilt," James said, squirming.

"The hilt was almost inside of her body."

James unclasped his hand from the pencil. It fell to the table and rattled. "Do you know where I can find him?"

"If he ain't at Kroc Houses, he's at the McDonald's up on LaSalle."

"He's a fast food junkie?"

"I guess you could say that. But he don't be eating it. He owns a piece of the place. That's why he calls the apartments Kroc Houses."

"In honor of Ray Kroc?"

"Yeah, he's obsessed with the dude. He made us all read a book about him. He went to the Hamburger College."

James nodded. He knew what she was talking about, had heard about "Hamburger University," the famed McDonald's management school that taught would-be franchisees the nut-and-bolts of running their own restaurant. James put the notepad and pencil back in his jacket, and listened as Conchita continued.

"All this useless shit that he wanted us to learn, like McDonald's sells however many billion burgers a year, and girls got to make their quotas 'cause hoeing is a franchise just like fast food." She shook her head, marveling at the memory of perverse motivational seminars, some tenuous capitalistic bond between selling her body and selling Happy Meals that God Body Divine had wanted to establish and sear into their brains.

James stood up. The girl slowly rose to her feet. The detective spoke. "Priority number one is finding out what happened to Amy, but if it comes down to it, would you be afraid to take the stand and face God in court?"

"Nah." she shook her head and laughed. "He made five-hundred thousand off me being on my back, if he made a dollar. And I don't even have money to fix my tooth." She smiled and pointed at her gap.

"Your teeth look fine. Good luck with getting your gig here when you're done."

"Yeah, thanks."

He walked toward the door, grabbed the brass doorknob. "Listen," Conchita said, "if God says he doesn't know where she was on the day she went missing, he's lying. He might not know where she is now. But he knows where he sent her that day."

James took his hand off the knob, puzzled. "Why do you say that?"

"Remember, Ghetto Ray Kroc is on top of his game. He keeps a little book where he writes where we went, how much we made, everything. If you hit a casino and make ten grand in a night, and you buy a Baby Ruth, God wants the receipt that says ninety-nine cents."

James nodded, opened the door for her, and followed her back into the lobby of "Breaking Out."

Chapter Nine

Wyoming was shaping up to be a land of brown hills and gray valleys, and not the level stretch of green grass and farmland that Amy imagined up until now whenever she heard the state mentioned.

"I haven't even seen a single cow."

Aaron grunted. Amy continued looking out of the window for a moment. She set her feet on the dashboard and stared out through the massive window. A stampede of gray clouds flitted across the sky. She imagined them as solid masses, not as moisture, and pictured a giant acrobat flitting from cloud to cloud, each of the cottony billows so dense, rich, and interconnected that it was possible to see the painted gymnast in her mind dancing from one side of the sky to the other without leaving the cloudbank.

She had always been like this. Coke didn't enhance one's imagination. It just made their observations seem more profound. She didn't want to talk to the burly trucker, which left her only to hatch thoughts in her mind and then to congratulate herself on her profundity.

"How long do we have to reach California?" She asked.

"Three days," Aaron said, steering toward an invisible line somewhere in the distance. He had his own fantasies of this country, and when he watched the sides of the road he imagined streams of Indians flowing down into the valley. They would be mounted on spotted Percherons, wearing feathered headdresses and holding spears, with bone plate armor latticed across their chests, whooping and hollering for white scalps.

He wasn't exactly sure whether or not the Paiutes and Osage who once inhabited this valley actually wore feathered headdresses or whooped for white scalps, but it was his fantasy, and the incongruity of running down savages with his bobtail rig struck him as somehow funny.

It was so funny that he laughed out loud, breaking the wall of his imagination and inviting Amy to look at him askance, before returning to her own thoughts.

She took in the view outside of her rain-streaked window. There was finally some green appearing, a nearly phosphorescent skin of moss hugging the backs of the hills which rose and fell together like a pack of slowly-migrating turtles, beneath which there was only a vast abyss it was best not to contemplate. Other than the thin layer of lichen, there were only a few ponderosas dotting the slopes and crests of the mounds, but the scant trees made no more impression than a few errant barnacles on the hull of giant ship. This land belonged to the hills, and not to the trees, or the trucks, or to the metal insects crawling over their insignificant channels.

Amy turned her attention back to the cab. She wished she had some gum, or some nail polish for her toes, something to occupy her time. "Are we going to need gas soon?"

Aaron checked his gauges. "We'll stop for a minute in Rock Springs," he said, and then returned his eyes, inscrutable behind his mirrored red shades, back to the road. Amy thought he saw all the way to Sacramento, California, and could probably divine mice flitting in the short grass like a hawk.

She had to give it to him. He was creepy bastard, but he was a master truck driver. "Are we going to Colorado?"

Aaron shrugged. "It's a little bit out of our way, but we might."

"Is there snow on the mountains there year-round?" She was hoping Colorado would not be as much of a letdown as Wyoming had been.

"On the caps. Yeah, most of that isn't really snow, though. It's glaciers."

"What's the difference?"

He sighed. "Listen, why don't you go play around in the berth for a little while?"

She took the hint, stood, and left him to fend off the raiding parties forming in his mind's eye. Amy sliced her hands between two dangling sheets of bamboo bead curtains and walked into the back. It was impossible to get over how awesome it was in the sleeper berth, the button tuck interior, the shaggy floors, and the soundproof walls covered in a velour-like cloth that resembled coffin pleating.

When she was alone back here it was as if her soul had survived death, and now inhabited some plush purgatory that was better than heaven. It would have made a perfect love nest, if she'd had a boyfriend, or it would have been quite the hangout spot, if she'd had a friend with whom to share it. The truth of the matter, though, was that Aaron Neblett was neither her friend nor her lover. The possibility that he might try to screw her had been permanently squelched by an admission he made the last time they had stopped, at a Flying J gas station to fill up on diesel.

They'd stood there and shared a bag of Stuckey's seasoned pecans, and after Aaron had licked the cinnamon dust from his fingers, he came right out of the holster with, "You don't have think about me jumping your bones. I am of the opinion that a woman without a penis isn't a woman at all. So unless you grow a she-cock sometime, you can relax."

As gross as that was to her, it was yet another sign of his forwardness. He had no respect for her, but clearly also had no desire to bullshit her, either. She could live with this, provided the coke held out. As things stood, the condom was down to a fingernail's worth collecting in the reservoir tip of the Trojan. She got the remainder into her nose by turning the latex inside out and working her finger against the head of the condom, pressing the rubber against what cartilage remained on the inside of her nostrils.

"Oh, God," she moaned.

The carpet moved beneath her. The walls and floor of the sleeper radiated with an atomic warmth, a lysergic blend of pastels and nuclear lava floating in a psychedelic lamp, where she was just an amoeba of colored wax, a blob floating and joining other happy orbs bouncing from one side of their mating ground to the other.

She went into the standing-room-only lavatory, and watched her nose for a telltale flow of blood. That had always been a problem for her with good coke, but her nostrils were dry and it was apparent that the mucous membranes in her nose had finally gotten acclimated to the Peruvian flake.

Amy gathered whatever residue remained on the condom, foraging with adept fingers that worked as manically as those of a sweatshop worker. She ran her coked index finger around her gums vigorously like a toothbrush, until she couldn't feel the front of her face. The truck lurched a bit, and her head flew against the mirror, making a loud thudding sound. She felt nothing and laughed, righted herself and came out of the bathroom.

She breathed deeply, and passed back through the bamboo bead partition separating the cab from the sleeper. She sat back down in the passenger seat and folded her hands in her lap. She dreaded having to ask Aaron for anything, but knew the time was rapidly approaching when she would have to ask. It would kill her buzz (to the extent that anything could kill the one she had going), and would reestablish a link of dependence between them, solve once again who was master and who was slave. She had nothing with which to bribe or control him, she knew, except her presence, which satisfied him in some ambiguous way that he wasn't able to explain. She wasn't going to be able to "grow a she-cock" as Aaron had so colorfully put it, so that didn't leave her much. She could perhaps control him with the threat that she might leave, but then he might kill her, or see through her ruse, recognize that if she fled he could bring her back with a line of white powder to ensnare her as easily as salt could trick a deer into a blind, where it would lick and mince until the hunter pulled the trigger.

"Do you want me to put something in your ass?" She said. "I've done it before."

Aaron glanced at her, returned his eyes to the road, and shook his head. "I don't have any dildos."

"We could use a toothbrush. Or the back of a comb." She didn't mention her fingers, and hoped he would leave that off the table. The coke was good, but not *that* good. If she touched his prostate right, she thought, if she hit that magical button that women had in front and men had in back, maybe she could gain some measure of control over him.

Aaron shook his head, more emphatically this time. His shoulder length dusty hair flowed from side to side, making his satin company jacket rustle a bit. "I've tried it, even got a lot lizard to use a strap-on on me, a little vibrating egg, too."

Coke made any sexual act better, but she hesitated to tell him that, fearing that he might take a toot, decide he liked it, and cease to give her a daily ration. That was what it was, now that she thought about it, a daily bowl of food for the resident dog, a mere trickle of water for the hamster. That was what made the asking so degrading, humiliating. Once the question was out, she couldn't stand the little sly smile that might appear on his face. She hated to be controlled by men, whether the man was this weird trucker or the God Body Divine himself.

"It's not the same," Aaron said. "It has to be a she-male. No transvestites and no girls with toothbrushes."

They were approaching a tunnel, the red vaporous track lights on the ceiling of the concrete burrow beckoning them, a portal into a cave beneath the green hill that had once been a mountain. There was a ripping sound, the rush of air as they were momentarily underground and the narrow walls around them roared.

"Aren't you worried about hitting the top of your truck when you go through one of these?"

He regarded her differently, as if she was no longer a nuisance, the little girl. For once, she realized, she had asked a question which he hadn't considered a mere momentary imposition, the buzzing of an annoying bee to be swatted away before continuing on with the picnic.

"There was a sign on the tunnel which tells you the clearance. The clearance on that tunnel was thirteen-five, meaning thirteen feet, five inches."

"How high is your cab?"

"Twelve-six."

She nodded. "But sometimes," he said, "especially when road conditions are bad, you have to account for that. Say there was some heavy snow and there's ice all over the top of your truck, and on the ceiling of the tunnel."

"Yeah, but ice just breaks."

"Yeah, and ice also gets hard, really hard. It can cause problems, scrape the top of your cab. Remember, it's just made of fiberglass. And hale and rocks and all kinds of crap get stuck in the ice on top of the tunnel. Understand?"

Amy nodded. Aaron wondered if he could teach her to drive, maybe prep her to get her own CDL. That was the kind of thing that friends did for each other. He envisioned himself showing her things, how to fill out a logbook, how to shift, how to apply snow chains (which they might actually have to do on this trip).

"Can I have some more coke?"

Aaron turned to her. She batted her eyes, which grew moony, a pleading pout on her fishy lips. "You already went through that bag?"

She huffed, stomped her feet in the floorboard, and looked out of her window. "I knew he was going to be like this," she muttered, ostensibly to herself but deliberately loud enough for him to hear it. She glanced over. He was watching her, his own eyes now pleading. She suppressed a smile.

"All right. When we stop."

That hadn't gone how he'd planned it. He had prepared for the inevitable moment when she would ask for more, and had thought he would set down some ground rules, let her know that she couldn't just steamroll over him, and that she had to pace herself. He was no drug dealer, and had no Triple-Beam scale with which to parse out and dole the Peruvian Flake. He in fact knew very little about much besides trucks, but even with his limited knowledge of the drug world he knew that she was going too fast through dope that was too strong, and that if he acquiesced like this, time and again, he would have a dead girl on his hands, one he hadn't planned for and one he would have to bury somewhere among these green hills.

It was too late to back out now, however. Next time he would set some firm limits. Aaron hadn't been ready this time, hadn't been prepared for that endearing pout and those pleading eyes. He had not braced himself for the rush of warm joy that had accompanied the realization that he was in control of her happiness. He had been in control before, but only in control of several thousand pounds of bison, a big rig, and at one point some lower-enlisted soldiers back when he was in the Corps. This was a person, a young and beautiful girl.

"Next time we stop." Aaron resumed his focus on the road. When he had traded out the Kenworth for the Volvo, he switched the remaining seventeen bags of dope from the headache rack of the former to the cab guard of the latter. The drugs were locked safely away and the key was on a dog-tag chain around his neck (along with a custom tag that said "Semper Fi" and was plated in gold). If she put two and two together and got any ideas, and managed to make off with the cocaine, he knew that she was going to run away, and that he would again be friendless and alone, driving the last leg to California with no one by his side to pester him with their questions, or to distract him with their scent coming in light waves, a breezy lavender and warm lilac that made him feel like he was her Uncle Aaron and she his niece, named...what he asked himself. *Jennifer.*

Through the window, the hills finally rose high enough to be called mountains, having cast off their light green dust, showing their rocky formations which jutted out, and brandishing layers much like a marbleized slab of well-cut Kobe beef, each slice distinguished one from the other. The mountains showed their age like the massive redwood trees of California, but unlike the trees one did not have to hew any staves to stare at the rings and appreciate their ancientness. Their majesty was plain and naked for both the driver and his passenger to see, but neither bothered to look.

Amy was busy thinking about coke, and Aaron was busy playing cowboys and Indians in his mind, his rig a Conestoga with a canvas bow top rolling along a trail. "This is Injun country," he said out loud, again surprising himself by breaking the proscenium arch behind which he kept his thoughts and secrets.

"What?" A chupacabra was gnawing through the synapses of her brain. It said "Coke, coke, coke, cokecokecoke" and "More coke."

Aaron changed the subject. "You want to go to the casino?"

Chapter Ten

One spin around the Kroc Houses after sunset let Detective Arklow know that it would not be prudent to go looking for God at night. Kroc was not a public housing complex, but it had the same nondescript layout as a project, and there was a sign notifying potential renters that HUD vouchers were accepted. As a place where people lived, it should have been intimate, but was about as welcoming as a public high school, and as formidable a structure as the local general hospital. Any white man walking through there alone at night would have inhabited one of three unambiguous categories: addict, cop, or clueless mark, and violence was assured if someone read him wrong and James was forced to shoot. It was better to wait.

He took the rest of the night off, returned to the Extended Stay, and set the alarm clock for six am the next morning.

Around sunrise, he got dressed, switched his air-weight .38 from hip to shoulder holster, and headed down to the McDonald's franchise where Conchita said that God Body Divine was part-owner.

There was very little chance of seeing the pimp this early in the morning, he knew. Gentlemen of leisure were not known to rise with the sun. God was more than likely asleep in one of the units of his affordable housing complex. James nevertheless kept an eye out for a heavyset black man who wore sweaters with florid patterns and kept shoulder-length dreadlocks. He finished his Egg McMuffin, had two cups of scalding black coffee, and then headed back to Kroc Houses.

The picnic area and basketball court fronting the building were empty, save for a young black couple pushing a stroller. They wore matching kufis and tricolor African pendants on leather thongs around their necks. James got out of his car, grazed the impression of his pistol hidden beneath his khaki windbreaker, and walked down the concrete path leading toward the front of the building.

The mortar face of Kroc Houses was bare, except for a few errant cracks and the odd air-conditioning unit or potted plant gracing otherwise empty windowsills. The Afrocentric couple glanced up at the lone white man violating their sanctum, and then they turned their attention back to their baby. A small claque of pigeons swarmed around them as they searched for bread, and the husband swatted them away while the baby cooed and held out his outstretched arms toward the birds he was too young to loathe, as was the birthright of every city dweller. The birds departed, flapping off toward better purchase among pensioners on benches and joggers in parks.

Directly ahead there was a breezeway lying in shadow, the kind of blind spot in an already-intimidating structure that would have given everyone from pizza men to police officers pause when they were called to come out here. James thought he could distinctly hear the sound of an infant crying as he moved closer to the breezeway. He turned around quickly, searching for the couple with the stroller, thinking as he spun that perhaps through some trick of acoustics the baby threw its voice as it moaned.

When he finally did spot the child between his parents, the babe was as docile as he had been before. Besides that, the cries he heard sounded like they came from an older child, not yet able to say words, but already forming its syllables into something approximating speech. James ducked under the breezeway, toward the sounds of the crying baby. An open newspaper carried on a light wind, its fish wrap folds splashing open and crumpling against his legs as he attempted to kick the thin sheets away.

When he finally did manage to disentangle himself from the paper, he saw that it was the *Amsterdam News.* The banner headline announced: "Black Athena Rising: The African Roots of Antiquity." The accompanying caption featured the scholar John Henrik Clarke, pointing an accusatory finger toward an opposite accompanying caption that showed both King Tut and Jesus Christ with thin European features.

James turned right, toward the sounds of the crying baby. He saw it in the grass, wearing only a diaper and moaning. It was a boy, his forehead creased and his mouth an uneven line of toothless flesh, out of which hellish sounds emanated. The boy wore only a diaper, the cold wind lapping at his pudgy drumstick-like legs and making him miserable. The baby walked across a small concrete pad, and pressed his hands against the glass of a sliding door that led to an apartment unit. He touched the pane with his snotty nose and left an imprint, and then turned around.

The baby saw James, perplexed for a moment. He struggled to form words with his mouth, let out a garbled syllable, exhausting his vocabulary in a guttural noise that lasted until he ran out of breath. James looked around for a parent, a guardian, any adult, and saw no other living being around them, save for two pigeons perched on separate spikes of a black aluminum fence. They cooed at each other.

James went over to the baby and picked him up, holding him in his arms. He shook him from side to side, forming a cradle in his elbows, making shushing sounds as he rocked him to sleep. The baby grew quiet, and the sliding door at the back of the apartment building swung open.

"Hey, devil, keep your pink fingertips off my seed."

James turned toward the voice, saw God Body Divine standing there. He was dressed casually, that rare ghetto shot caller who was not ostentatious, whose power came from nothing that could be tangibly understood by a white man, or even a bourgeois black one. He was big, but the muscle and fat were deceptively intertwined so that one could neither describe him as muscular or fat. He was only formidable, the single sign of his human frailty some salty streaks at the tips of his knotty dreads. He wore a black t-shirt with a negative image of track-and-field gold medalist John Carlos throwing up a black power fist at the 1968 Olympic Games.

"God Body Divine?" He felt silly saying it, but knew the man probably would not respond to any other name.

God nodded slightly, acknowledging he was one and the same. "Do you know you have a naked baby in your backyard?"

"That ain't a baby," God said. "That's my seed. And I suggest you put him down, before I righteously fuck you up. Can you comprehend that, swine merchant?"

"I comprehend." James kept his voice soft and calm, as he put the child down onto its feet. "The seed born of your wisdom, right?"

God seemed like he was thrown off balance for a moment. It was probably the only point he would be scoring all afternoon, James noted. The baby walked toward his father, its arms outstretched and anticipating a lift into the authority of his dad's arms. His father rudely brushed him into the darkness of the apartment unit behind him. "Kendra!" he shouted. "Watch Kamal!"

He turned back to the white man. "What do you know about the knowledge?"

"My buddies took down a compound filled with Five-Percenters running guns in Steubenville, Ohio, a few years back."

"Yeah, I heard about that," He seemed momentarily wary, but unimpressed. For James, it had been time to make a split decision. Either brandish his law enforcement credentials to possibly gain some footing and risk the chance that God would shut down altogether, or continue to be considered nothing but a joke, some blindly lost white man, possibly here on a domestic call to investigate allegations of child abuse or something of that nature.

God hadn't shut the glass sliding door, so there was obviously still a chance to find something out. "Clarence Thirteen Ex," James said. Best to keep talking shop about religion. Supposedly T.E. Lawrence had gotten his toehold in the Ottoman Empire by quoting the Quran in Arabic to a local Bedouin warlord. "He was in the Nation of Islam, had an epiphany when he was in Bellevue Hospital for psychiatric evaluation. That was where he formulated his idea of the Gods in the Earth."

"Yeah, all right. You're a sly devil. I'll give you that. But see, I stay ecumenical. I believe either the path discovered by Elijah Muhammad, or

Khalid Muhammad, or Brother Clarence is all righteous. It all leads to the knowledge of self."

Another child, an older son, appeared behind God. He swung a Nerf baseball bat, taking wide Mattingly-like swings against his father's kneecaps and getting an unresponsive foam thud for all his troubles. "Know what this is?"

"Let's see. The other one is your yard kid, and this is your house kid?"

"You got jokes, but it won't be funny in Twenty Forty-Three."

"What happens then? The end of the world?" He wasn't up on the latest in pseudo-Muslim theology. He could see why Malcolm X had finally renounced the black American variant of Islam, repudiating it for the Sunni sect.

"It'll be the end of your world," God said, wrapping his massive hand around the contours of his son's head. "That's when you devils become a minority in this country. It won't be quite so fun when the rabbit has the gun and the hunter's on the run. Now, will it?"

"I'll be long dead."

"Yeah." God smiled, perhaps contemplating the death of a white man, any white man, savoring the outcome even should it be by natural causes. "So what do you want?"

"Well," James said, cracking his knuckles as he spoke, just in case he had to make a fast play for the .38. He didn't want to miss God and end up hitting the wife or the kids, if it came to that. "I'm a private detective. I was planning on putting together an elaborate ruse before I came over here. A disguise, an identity, the works."

God watched him, perplexed. The pimp's older son lost interest, and disappeared back into the house screaming after his younger brother. "You see, I was going to pretend to be a John, tell you that one Amy Loeher beat me out of my money and that I would be willing to cut you in on some of it if you could tell me where she was."

"You couldn't have gotten that by me. I'm not susceptible to deception, and you smell too much like an Officer Overseer to me, anyway."

"Right, so I figured why bother anyway, right?" He smiled widely. "I mean, I've got a girl in protective custody, seventeen years old, says you've been pimping her and other underage girls for the last couple of years, washing your money through this place, writing their trick money off on the books as rent payments." James held out his hands. "This is quite an impressive operation. You are an entrepreneur of the first order."

"Okay." The veneer of holiness, of righteous racial anger had evaporated. He squirmed slightly, looked over his beefy shoulder toward the family with whom he wanted to remain, at the home and the life he would have to leave if he went to prison. "What do you want? How does five grand strike you?"

James shook his head. "I don't want money. I want you to look through those elaborate books you keep, and I want you to tell me where Amy Loeher went on the day she went missing."

"Snow bunny," God said, a frown of contempt pulling his lips downward, as if he just drank pure brine. "She made a good grip, but she was more trouble than she was worth. I put so much work into that bitch. She was a Choosey Susie, too. She went from one pimp to another until I finally broke her ass for good."

"Yeah." James recalled what the girl had told him. "You broke her pretty good." He took a deep breath, repressing the rising anger. He wanted to pull out the air-weight, pistol whip him because he knew that no matter how big God was, he was a pimp and most, if not all, pimps were natural cowards. He wanted to beat the man in front of his wife and kids. But if he did that, it was doubtful the man would lead him to the girl.

"Tell me where you sent Amy Loeher the night she disappeared. You do that and I'll go away. If you don't tell me, I'm going to get my little songbird up on a stand to sing her little Aria for a jury of twelve angry men, all of them fathers with little daughters at home."

"All right." God's voice was almost a whisper and he blinked repeatedly, muttering, "I got the picture. I don't need an oil painting."

"Good."

"Come on in." God slid the glass sliding door further open and James followed him inside. The house smelled of comingling oils and incense, a rich cocoa buttery tone melding with the life-affirming scent of frying fish. There were several flags on the walls. A Jamaican, Haitian, and

Liberian one were displayed prominently, and they were the only ones James could identify by sight. The room they now entered was dark except for a massive fish tank that gave the room a purple cast. The percolating sound of bubbles forming and then popping was a gentle music that played counterpoint to the echoing noise of two children fighting, and their mother scolding them somewhere off in another room of the house.

The two men finally came to the backroom, where the décor made a sharp detour into the Eurocentric. There were prominent framed pictures of both Ray Kroc and Sam Walton. A wraparound desk with a varnished wood grain surface bisected the room. Two computers and a phone were on top of the desk, along with several copies of a book: *Grinding It Out,* by Ray Kroc. None of these furnishings, James noticed, would have been out of place in a corporate boardroom, or in a lawyer's office. The only indication that a gangster lived and did his work here was the cane and wicker chair where a Kalashnikov rifle rested on one side, and a Bushmaster AR-15 lay on the other side. Both had extended banana magazines fed into them, and James guessed it was a good bet that both weapons had rounds chambered.

God Body Divine was running his fingers through alphabetized manila folders, each separated one from the other by protruding Post-It notes. "I doubt if you put Conchita on the stand she would hold up under cross-examination. I got a Semite, a precious metal-stein from Hymietown by the name of Goldberg. It's like what Sharpton said. This Jew pins his Yarmulke back and he can eat any case that gets thrown at me." God found the file, pulled it out, and continued talking. "The bitch is a hoe, a proven drug addict, who's lied to the cops before. My lawyer will eat her ass up under cross-examination."

"Maybe, but I've checked your jacket out. You've never so much as been charged with jaywalking. You really want to break your streak right now? Even if you win, you're on their radar forever."

God sighed. "I wish you'd just taken a bribe," he said, opening the file. James studied God's hands as the man thumbed through the papers inside, noticing that his fingers were done over in clear varnish, perfectly manicured except for the thumb and pinky, which had been allowed to grow well past the length of the other fingernails.

James picked up the Ray Kroc biography from the desktop. He read: "...frying time to suit the balance of water to solids in a given batch of potatoes."

"That book will change your life. Did you know one in eight Americans has been employed by McDonald's at some point in their life?"

"I did not know that. But I do now."

"Yep, if McDonald's was a country, it would have the world's sixty-eighth largest economy."

"Amy. Where was she that night?"

"Here." God pointed to a line on his ledger. At the beginning of each margin there was her code name, "Snow Bunny," where she had been "deployed" (God's words), how much she had earned (number of "roses"), as well as her time of return (written in military time, i.e. "1200 Hours"). The fields on each line were filled in until James ran his finger to the last one, where every field was filled in except for the return time. The location was a truck stop about fifteen minutes outside of city limits.

"Like I said," God said, "she was a handful. Not only a Choosy Susie, but her mama reported her as a runaway after I already had her with me for a while. The cops were out in force looking for her, so I couldn't just send her to the regular track, where she might get picked up by the police or get spotted by someone who knew her. It ain't my fault she disappeared. After her mama put that missing persons report out on her, I had no choice but to send Amy to sketchy joints out of town, where I didn't know the lay of the land. Mama said her daughter was missing, and at the end of the day mama Maggie made it so. If Amy'd been down at the regular hoe stroll, she would have been close to home where I could keep an eye on her, because they know down there not to steal my merchandise."

"She's not your merchandise."

"Yeah, well, she was. If you want my opinion, some Ed Gein type of cracker hillbilly motherfucker got a hold of her, probably made a lampshade out of her ass."

"You'd better hope not," James said, copying the address of the truck stop from God's ledger into his little notepad. "If I find her and she's dead when I get to her, I'll do everything in my power to make you an accessory. And if her body's found out of state, I'll try to add an interstate trafficking beef enhancement to the charge."

"Why? You told me you just wanted to know where she went that night. It's all there." He nodded toward the file, his graying dreads shaking as his head fluttered.

"Yeah, I know. I'm a liar."

"I should have known. Yakub, the bearer of a thousand diseases, all vile and disgusting. A curse upon the Earth."

"Look who's talking." James left the file on the table, folded the little notepad closed, sandwiched his pencil stub between the spirals of his tiny book, and placed the pad back inside the pouch of his khaki windbreaker, opposite the pocket where he kept his air-weight .38.

"I'm a father figure. I provide the steadying hand for a bitch who's lost her way."

James looked at him, wondering for a moment if he actually believed that. It was certain that he could get the girls to believe it. God was not in fact the worst pimp that Detective Arklow had run across in his investigations, as hard as that was to believe. He had known one, Redbone, who was worse. When Redbone deemed a girl's performance subpar after a night of "flat-backing," he would occasionally boil a pot of water, place a penny at the bottom of the pot, and force the underperforming prostitute to attempt to extract the penny. He called this his "Trial by Water." Still, James regarded God as an exceptionally shitty human being.

God watched the detective now, and perhaps sensing the judgment the man was passing, spoke. "It's not too late. Ray Kroc was in his fifties before he got started with McDonald's. The same was true for Harlan Sanders and KFC. This black God is only thirty-three years young."

The detective shook his head, and God averted his eyes, the dreads falling in his face, his gaze on his manicured fingers, and the hands with which he beat women. "It's not too late," the pimp said.

But they both knew that his soul had departed long ago, that it had flown wherever that holy ether levitated to when a man crossed that final threshold. Still, there was an ugly knowledge forming in the detective's mind as he walked back through the fish and cocoa-butter smelling apartment, this unpleasant thought taking up residence and forcing him forward, back out through the sliding glass door, across the pavement to his car waiting in front of Kroc Houses

The thought which so propelled him was this: however bad God was, however despicable the impression the pimp made, he knew the odds were good that God Body Divine was nowhere near as bad as the man that had Amy Loeher at this moment.

Chapter Eleven

The crowning feature of the last rest stop before they reached the Indian reservation was a plaster mockup of a lighthouse. It was fixed into the center of the roof of the main building, where the bathrooms and vending machines were housed alongside a massive wall-length map. They were reaching the territory skirting the Pacific Northwest, but the lighthouse was more a vestige of New England, and the gray cast to the sky made it easy for Aaron to imagine he was rolling along the eastern Atlantic coastal highway.

"What kind of trees are those?" Amy said, hopping down from the cab. Her legs were unsteady, and she felt weak. She also felt dirty. She had taken a shower in the sleeper berth's bathroom, but the water pressure was low and the truck shook from side to side on the road as she attempted to wash herself. Aaron had said that bobtailing was harder than driving with a rig, because at least with a rig there was something to keep the truck's weight on the road. Without the rig, the tractor just got tossed from side to side like a sailboat on an angry sea.

"Those?" He saw a few smaller trees hugging the slope of a low hill, nesting at the edge of an old-growth forest where the subalpine giants hovered above them. "Those are Douglas Firs."

"They look like Christmas trees." She touched the tips of her fingers underneath either of her armpits, and then put them up to her nose for a tentative sniff. Then she rubbed her scalp with the palm of her hand. She shifted her purse from one arm to the other.

"Yeah, they are Christmas trees. Listen, I'm going to check the gators. Why don't you go inside? Get something from the vending machine."

They had snacks and little vittles in the truck, but she knew what he meant. He wanted her to screw off for a few minutes so that he could get another bag of coke without her finding out where he kept it hidden.

"Okay."

The rest stop building was made of massive quarry rock columns, its top shaped like a Japanese daimyo. A battery of glowing Coke machines provided the only light, save for when someone opened one of the bathroom doors and momentarily splashed the dark atrium with a sickly fluorescence. Amy ducked under the shadowed canopy, removed a pocket mirror applicator from her purse. She held it in front of her face as if she was about to apply her Claiborne lipstick.

In the small oval of glass she saw a man with a beard, a company hat, and matching company jacket. He was climbing on the back of his Volvo truck cab, taking a key from around his neck, and inserting it into the cab guard. That was all she needed to see. Amy slammed her applicator case shut the next moment and headed for the women's bathroom.

There was only one other person in there, a frumpy middle-aged woman with a kitten made from golden sequins sewn onto her sleeveless black shirt. She struggled to put her contacts in as she looked in the mirror. Several insects- a conclave of gnats, flies, and moths- struggled on the edge of a transom, where they made hideous flapping noises as they fluttered. Amy walked into the one of the foul smelling stalls, calling bullshit silently to herself on that old myth about women's bathrooms being better maintained than men's.

She balanced herself on the edge of the toilet seat, placed the makeup applicator back in her purse, and took out her cellphone. She turned it on for the first time in weeks. Amy ignored the thirty-three missed calls, skipped right to "Contacts," and brought up God himself, after hitting only "G" and triggering the autocomplete feature.

It rang twice. "'Lo?"

Amy could hear Kendra in the background, laughing at an episode of *Sanford & Son.* "I'm finally back online, daddy."

"No, you ain't." His voice was full of scorn. She feared his fists, the violence of his reprisals, even over the distance afforded by hundreds of miles. "You're still out of pocket on me."

“I’m working an angle right now. I got this trick’s nose all the way open.”

God Body Divine took a deep breath. “How open?”

“Fully sprung. He’s got some pure lemonhead white.”

“How much?”

Amy laughed. “A bunch.” She didn’t know how to measure dope when it was in condoms.

“I don’t see what’s so amusing.” His voice had softened. Amy knew his mannerisms well enough to know that he was cupping the phone with his hand, trying to filter out the distraction of his wife watching sitcoms on a couch in the other room. Kendra was the only woman he respected. “All right. Do what you’ve got to do to redeem yourself in the eyes of God. Hit that lick. Get daddy his money, or his dope.”

Amy faltered. God had never used the word “dope” over the phone, or even in person, since as long as she had known him. He thrived on euphemisms, partly because of the respect that they could afford him, since “International Playboy” sounded better than “Pimp,” but he did it mainly in order to stay out of trouble with the cops.

“What’s wrong?” Amy asked.

That momentary pause was more than enough to answer her question. Everything was wrong, obviously. Had he been operating from a place of strength, he would have put her in check the moment she had asked him a question. A pimp’s thoughts and feelings were his own divine provenance. A woman could massage his shoulders to give him some relief, but that was as far as she could encroach upon his world. Kendra had more latitude, since she was his Wisdom, and he her God, but that was an exception.

"I got problems," God said. "We got problems."

"Like what?"

"There's a detective looking for you. Your mama put him onto you."

"Shit."

There was a knock on the bathroom door. It startled Amy so that she almost dropped the phone into the toilet. She looked up, through the crack in her stall. The door to the bathroom was now halfway open, and the bill of a mesh trucker filled the doorway.

"God, I got to go." She hung up before she could hear his response, her action the very epitome of being 'out of pocket,' the kind of disrespectful transgression that could have gotten her beaten into a coma under different circumstances. But these were not normal circumstances, and she was more frightened of Aaron Neblett than she was of God Body Divine. In fact, the nicer he was to her, the scarier this all became.

"You ready?" he asked.

"Yeah," she said, fumbling with a nervous hand on the toilet paper roll, pulling sheet after sheet and making enough noise to hopefully fool him into thinking she had been using the bathroom. "I'll be out in a moment."

"All right."

The door closed and she heaved a sigh. She turned her phone off, threw it into her purse, and went back out into the main area of the rest stop. A couple with a canoe tied to the rack of their station wagon had pulled in next to their truck while she had been in the bathroom. They played catch with their Labrador, throwing a Frisbee through the air, while the handkerchief-clad pure breed tried to catch it before it hit the ground.

Amy fell in alongside Aaron as he walked back toward the truck. "What are gators?" she asked.

"Huh?"

"You said you had to 'check the gators.' "

"Oh, that's trucker slang. Gators are truck tires. I had to check the tread depth and the air."

"What if something is wrong?"

Aaron stopped in front of the truck. He kicked the cast aluminum rim of one of the tires. "These are Dayton wheels. I don't have any recaps on me, and I wouldn't want to try to change a tire on someone else's rig."

"So what would we do?"

"I'd call in to Dispatch on my Qualcomm and I'd get directions to the nearest mechanic who's approved to work on big rigs."

Aaron held Amy's door open for her. He didn't try to give her an assist, as that would have involved touching her. She struggled upward. "Three points of contact," he reminded her. "Remember to have three points of contact at all times."

"Got it."

Aaron walked around the cab to his side of the truck. He hopped up and started the key in the ignition.

"What kind of transmission is that?" She asked, pointing at all of the buttons arrayed on the left side of the massive steering wheel.

"This is an automatic ten-speed. It's about the easiest thing in the world to use."

Amy reached forward on the dash for the ledger with the black cover and the red spine. "What's this?"

"It's a logbook."

"But, I thought you had a log on this thing." She pointed at the hardened onboard computer.

"That is my logbook. But if the power goes out, I need a backup log, and that's what the paper log is for. It's a reserve, just in case I get pulled over by the DOT for an inspection. It's called 'C-Y-A.' Cover your ass. You ever heard of that?"

Amy shook her head. Aaron started the truck. The engine growled, and the sky ahead of them churned with a dark violence that spoke of the coming storm. "Do you think you could teach me to drive?"

"Might as well. If you're going to keep asking me these questions, there should be a reason."

Amy stood in the cab. She needed coke, and could tell she was annoying him. Both of their problems could be solved with only one gesture, and he knew it. She waited, said nothing, and kept her hands in her lap.

"Oh," Aaron said. He reached inside his jacket. She saw where the beaded metal chain slithered among the wooly tufts of his chest hair, and she knew the necklace held the key that could get her into that cab guard where the dope was hidden. If she could get in there, she would have enough to toot her way across the country, iced to the gills on a one-way Greyhound trip over the road, back into the arms of God, where she would still have enough Peruvian Flake left to break him off and make things right with daddy.

"Listen," Aaron said. "Why don't you go back there and get changed for dinner?"

"Where are we going?" She braced herself against the shimmering curtain of bamboo behind her.

"Casino, like I told you before. We're going to the Indian Reservation. We'll be there in twenty minutes or less. We'll do a little gambling, get some grub, and we'll spend the night in the suite. Sound good?"

"Yeah," Amy said, distantly.

"We'll be up and out of here by nine in the morning. We'll be in Nevada a little after Noon. We'll stop there for lunch."

"Okay," Amy said, and waited.

"Oh." Aaron glanced at the eggroll-sized bundle he held in his hand. "Go slower with this one."

Amy accepted the condom with the desperate gratitude of a wino receiving the last dollar needed for a bottle of muscatel. "Thank you," she said, brightly.

She almost skipped back through the beaded curtain, into what had formerly been her button-tuck dungeon, a crushed satin and velour prison where she felt withdrawal seeping in as it gnawed every fiber and nerve ending in her eyes and fingers, playing hell on her biorhythms, as if the drug controlled the thermostat inside of her. Without it she was destined for the torment of chills and hot sweats, tossing uncomfortably on a small bed in a cabin that was always moving down the road in a way that made her nauseous.

What a difference one line could make, though, sprinkled out and perfect, assuming the dimensions of one of her mom's Virginia Slim cigarettes. She blighted that fleeting thought of her aging mother, weighted with arthritis, years, and cat fur, and tugged with her nostrils until her effort smoothed the creases in her forehead.

Knives deployed by the white powder now proceeded to dice through her problems in waves. Nausea, fear, unhappiness, boredom, and other intangibles got sliced down into insignificance. Her heart beat like the wings of a bee pollinating a flower, with a purpose and a creative intensity that renewed the life inside of her. She smiled, danced, tried for a high kick but found the space too small, and planted her foot on the wall beside the bed.

The trucker barely visible through the curtain wasn't such a bad guy now. He was some misunderstood weirdo who was trying to make it all right, trying to atone for the wrong life he had lived, and she was his little karmic muse. Each time she took a hit of coke, it absolved him of some sin. Thus, she reasoned, she was his salvation.

Amy lay down on the carpet, found it as plush and shaggy as the coat of a caterpillar. It reminded her of the plastic green grass in the Easter baskets she got as a kid. She writhed on the carpet and waded, as if it was snow and she was making the form of an angel.

She thought back to earlier years at the Pentecostal church where she spent Sundays with her mother, before she was old enough to make a mistake or two with boys, before the whispers and stares had forever ruined Church and Jesus and everything else for her. Before the boys at school had made her so ashamed that for some reason she attempted to solve the pain by having sex with more men, as if that would show them, and hurt them, rather than her.

She closed her eyes, tried to remember the name of the man in the old Bible story who got swallowed by the whale. That's what this sleeper berth was, she thought, the belly of a whale. If she kept her eyes closed long enough, she could dissolve in here, disappear from the world and its problems as a bit of digested gristle.

Maybe this would work out. Aaron would teach her to become a truck driver. She would get her CDL, get all the endorsements he had been talking about, like for hazardous materials and whatnot, and she would finally be independent. She wouldn't need a pimp if she could earn money as an over-the-road trucker. She could even get a regional route, stay within one-thousand miles of home, which would give her a chance to go to Twelve Step meetings and kick the coke habit.

It was almost possible to believe it while this buzz lasted, while this radioactive ecstasy washed over her. It was all clear now: She would break free of her pimp and her addictions. She would get her commercial driver's license and she would go on to have a fulfilling career in trucking, complete with health benefits and optional employee stock options. She would take care of her mother in her old age.

Across from Amy, on the other side of the sleeper berth, there was the sundress she had bought from Mode O'Day's, the little vintage boutique in North Platte, Nebraska. It featured a pattern of crawling painted thorny roses at the hemline, above which there was an explosion of butterflies soaring toward the low cut neck. It was a beautiful dress.

Amy slithered out of her pants, pulled her top off, and unfastened her bra. She would go naked underneath the dress, she decided, keeping the cloth of the tie-dyed taffeta pulled close to her body. After changing, she went into the tiny water closet and gave herself a birdbath, using a roll-on deodorant applicator under her arms and gargling once with a full mini-bottle of mouthwash.

She grabbed the remaining dope, knotted the bag into a pretzel shape, and stuffed it down into her purse. By the time she had entered back into the front of the truck, it was as if they were in another country. A massive fingerboard sign to the side of the sandy road informed them both that they were now in "Beaverton Residential Living Community," whatever exactly that meant. The houses on either side of the road were primitive, and too dull in color and structure to reveal in passing whether or not they possessed running water or electricity. The neighborhood was like an especially depressed Amish village, whitewash saltbox houses, squat as the churches of a modest people who feared God's wrath in the wake of their vanity. Everything was chipped clapboard, the roofs caving and the porches sagging.

The people didn't look much better. There were little Indian boys who wore unseasonably hot sweaters, a parade of children dressed in the apparent hand-me-downs of white children. Their long black hair was coarse from the sand and grit, like the tails of Palomino horses. They squinted as they watched the truck pass them, perhaps shielding their eyes from the sun, or from the pains of hunger. One boy carried a massive stick and seemed to contemplate throwing it at the cab before they passed him by.

"What is this place?" Amy asked. She situated her purse on her lap and sat down in the passenger seat. Aaron had finally shown her how to adjust it for her weight, using the knobs on the side, and its heated Corinthian leather had memorized her contours. It was easy enough to fall asleep in it when she wasn't peaking on a buzz.

"This is the Res," Aaron said. He looked over. She had that look on her face, that perplexed expression, as if she was disappointed to have woken up and discovered gum in her hair. "This is the reservation, the biggest one in the country. Indian land." He decided he liked the sound of that.

He turned the rig left, a plain of glacial till soil spreading in front of their path, a massive glassy sheet of melt water expanding, catching the sun's reflection and forming a second sky across the length of the earth as far as the settlement stretched. They passed kitschy Indian trading posts that promised authentic Indian relics. They probably did not even bother to conceal the "Made in China" tags on the peace pipes, the beaded moccasins, and needlepoint.

They entered onto a theatrically overstated ghost town with false fronted buildings and batwing doors over the saloons, a place to "pan for gold," and a smoke shop with a cigar store Indian standing next to an old globe-topped gas pump next to a red "Enjoy Coca-Cola" sign.

Aaron was getting into the spirit of it, drumming his fingers at "10" and "2" on the steering wheel, whispering a few lines about the Marines at Montezuma and Tripoli, the Duke's war of attrition against the redskins somehow now merging in his imagination with his own troubles with the yellow men in the black pajamas back in the Ia Drang valley all those years ago. One good thing had come of his time in the 'Nam. He discovered lady boys at a Tiki-themed bar in Bangkok. Lady boys weren't exactly trannies, but one thing had led to another.

Amy sensed the change, and decided to ask him a question, if only to distract him from the thoughts forming in his head. "Where'd you hear about this place?"

Aaron laughed, whistled once through his parched lips. "Back in Seventy-One, a lot of boys was taking leave from the 'Nam and not coming back. Uncle Sam caught most of them, put them in Hoosegow either in LBJ or back in old Fort Leavenworth."

He looked over at her as he drove, saw the puzzled expression on her face, and provided a translation. "When I was in Vietnam, a lot of guys were running away, trying to escape from the War. Do you know what going AWOL is?"

A light went off, a temporary incandescence he knew wouldn't last very long. "Yeah, I know. My dad was in the Marines."

That struck Aaron, but he left her admission alone, and went on with his story. He'd come back to her and her dad in a minute. "Anyway, the MPS and CID were catching everybody, except one guy, Sergeant Begay. Know why the old Military Police and Criminal Investigation Division wasn't catching Sergeant Begay?"

Amy shook her head.

"Because he was an Arapaho Indian. When he beat feet out of the 'Nam, he had sense enough to head home to the Reservation. Uncle Sam's got a mighty long grip, but he couldn't reach out and touch Begay out here on the Res. He got away scot free, sent a postcard to all the grunts telling us he loved us, sent one to the noncoms telling them to kick rocks, and sent another one to the company commander telling him to kiss his red ass. Sergeant Begay wasn't nobody's Uncle Tomahawk no more."

The big, bearlike trucker laughed. Amy stared at him for a moment. That had been the longest stretch he had talked at one length in a while, and it was the first time he had shown anything approaching happiness, though she found his smile more unsettling than the bland expression he kept on his face whenever he was on the road, his brain humming in tune with the highway like a tuning fork striking an eternal and unchanging bass note. "Anyway, old Begay piqued my interest and once I had some time off to take a look for myself, I kind of got attached to the place. I try to make it out here whenever I can."

They drove past a cavernous hangar with four brick sides and a corrugated tin roof. To the side of the building was a massive red clay track with two rows of bleachers for the opposing teams. A giant, long-faced Indian mascot was painted between two unlit digital arrays on a scoreboard. The sign said: "Welcome to the Home of the Chiefs."

Beyond that, there was a campground where several tipis were erected and stood around the charred remains of a bonfire.

"What tribes are here?" Amy said.

"Mostly Shoshone and Arapaho. Maybe a little bit of Osage or Paiute."

"What's the difference?"

Aaron shrugged and decelerated. "I don't know. They all got their asses kicked by the white man, and now they run casinos."

Amy brightened. "Can I gamble?"

"What did your dad do in the Marines?"

Amy huffed, balking at the change in subject. "He was a DI at Paris Island. We lived at Camp Lejeune for a few years."

He seemed to accept that, mulled it over for a minute, and turned left into a blacktopped lot that covered at least several acres of ground. There were cars parked all the way to the entrance to the outer rim of the lot, a massive phalanx of four-doors, Winnebago motor homes, Minivans, and campers, all belonging to tourists eager to part with their white man's wampum. Aaron found a space for his truck that felt like it was half a mile from the entrance. They parked and chocked the wheels, and then they walked into the giant building.

The Wind River Indian Reservation Hotel and Casino was a massive combination of blockhouse and California mission décor, a Spartan and imposing fortress devoted to the glowing battery of whirring machines and green felt tables that spread across an earthy expanse whose interior felt like a massive walk-in humidor.

The industrial-grade carpet in the lobby was embroidered with topaz and jade patterns reminiscent of Indian totems and quillwork. It featured scenes of harvest, hunting, and migration, little animist gods with eagle heads and the muscled bronze bodies of fighting warriors. Various curios and tchotchkes were nailed to the walls, here a papoose for carrying babies, there a set of snowshoes. Much of it, Aaron decided, was probably revisionist kitsch which would easily pass the filter of the people in this lobby, who were too busy worrying about whether or not prime rib was on the buffet to notice this or that painting or sewn bit of patchwork cloth was something more common among the Mayans or Eskimos than among the Great Plains tribes.

Aaron himself couldn't have cared less, and momentarily felt as happy as "a dog with two peckers," as his father might have phrased it. It was a feeling that would not last, he knew, and so he didn't fight it.

He did a three-hundred and sixty degree inspection of the place, taking note of the dancing flames in the glassed-in fireplace, and the antlered-chandelier hanging from the ceiling. He wondered why he was suddenly thinking of the old man and his batch of colorful phrases. The answer hit him, as he queued and walked forward, how simple the association was and why he had remembered Aaron Senior.

He saw himself and his father together on the carpet, waiting for the Mandala of that old Indian test pattern to lift from the cathode face of the family's single channel Ambassador. They had gotten it cheap because his father was a salesman and this one had been a floor model, which meant it was used. They would watch some Matt Dillon, some *Gunsmoke*, some *Have Gun, Will Travel*, and maybe even an episode of *The Wild, Wild West.* Mama would be vacuuming in the background, aided by her little helpers not all that different from the "Yellow Jackets" that could keep a man's eyes peeled for forty-eight hours on a cross-country haul.

These were his memories, though, and since he didn't want to think of his mother as a pill head, he revised that misted image in his mind, replaced Susan Neblett with June Cleaver, and kept on trucking with the memory as he wanted to relive it.

Things weren't all that bad at the Neblett homestead right up until Kennedy's head burst like a pumpkin in the hands of a practical joker on Halloween, back before the Old Man bobtailed it for real and said he was going out for a pack of Chesterfields and left their lives, slinking across the country, and then finally slinking out of his mortal coil and this dimension when he put his old WWII Luger in his mouth and squeezed. Aaron Sr. had bragged after old Jack Kennedy got doled his ounce of lead that he had done his Basic Training in the same battalion as Lee Harvey, before Oswald had gone on to become a radar operator, and then on to infamy, when he shot the President of the United States from that book depository. The old man's left arm had borne an anchor & globe tattoo much like the faded Indian Ink relic which now danced on Aaron's own arm as he placed his credit card on the table, and smiled at the squaw with the two tight, raven braids: "A suite, please."

"I'm sorry, Sir," she said, glancing down to look at the screen of the little computer behind her desk. "All of our suites are booked up for the next two weeks. I can put you in the handicapped room, though."

Aaron thought about it for a moment, was about to ask how a handicapped room was a luxury, when the Arapaho woman said, "The bathroom is twice as large as a normal one. You have a perfect view of the golf course through your window. The bed is larger than a king size. You naturally have wireless and—"

"All right," Aaron looked at Amy. Her eyes were bright, sparkling, catching light from the fire and the chandelier. She was happy for the moment, he knew. She did not even mind his presence, and with another toot or two she maybe could even pretend to like him, which would have made him even more elated than he already was.

The receptionist quickly entered Aaron's information, printed a receipt, and handed him a keycard. "Thank you for staying at the Wind River Hotel," she beamed.

"Thank you." He smiled and doffed his trucker cap, before grabbing Amy lightly by the shoulder and pulling her down the hall. She neither resisted his touch nor fell into it. A bellhop, a young man with dream catcher earrings and a bolo tie, made for the couple but saw a moment later that they had no bags. He quickly turned around.

"Room's on the first floor," Aaron said, holding up the key card.

"Handicapped. It would have to be on the first floor."

Aaron slid the card from its white paper sleeve, giving it to her and keeping the remaining one for himself. They walked down the hall, past an activities room which had a dry erase board posted in the doorway, on which someone had written: "Learn Powwow etiquette, lore, and more here today at 2 p.m."

"No thank you," Aaron said.

"'No thank you,' what?"

"Nothing. Here...." Aaron pulled her by the hand, and stopped. To their left was a small espresso bar, its floor a checkered tile pattern, its counter and tables a rosined wood shellacked to a high shine. A few patrons sat at tables, taking advantage of the Wi-Fi Internet, while the barista, a Native who seemed incongruously masculine for his job, placed a green plastic stirring stick in a steamy double-shot and slid the tiny cup to a patron waiting on the other side of the glass bakery display.

Amy looked over to the little coffee shop, admiring the first real food and drink she had seen in weeks. Though the sleeper technically had the tools to cook, they had been living off edible simulacra at truck stops, the kind of fare that could crack the crown on one's tooth or leave them moored faithfully to the porcelain toilet for the duration of the road trip.

"I'm going to give you one-hundred dollars," Aaron said, and though she had been tuning him out, thinking of a bathroom bump to tide her through the evening, the mention of money brought her back to reality.

She held out her hand, took the smooth bill, and listened as he spoke. "Stay away from the tables because you don't know what you're doing. That goes double for video poker. Keep to the one-armed bandits."

"What are those?"

Aaron snorted and took her by the arm. "Come here."

They walked into the giant rotunda, the track lighting guiding them like movie patrons to their seats, or a plane along a darkened runway. The insect-like chirp of thousands of machines stealing money formed a counterpoint to the call of the few electric boxes that were paying out, coins spilling into their hoppers as the retirees with their oxygen tanks and tracheotomies gathered up their handfuls of semiprecious metal in paper cups where their Diet Dr. Pepper had sloshed a moment before.

A garish cornucopia of digital fruit fell, the vertiginous whir of colors and sounds making Amy sick with warm excitement. She had seen her mother get devoured by the empty hope provided by lottery tickets, her dreams dashed in the amount of time it took to scrape metal filings from a paper card with a rusted penny. Her mom had spent more than her fair share of time stroking the magenta or mint hair of a troll doll, that little devilish circle of kobolds she surrounded herself with in the basement of the Pentecostal church on bingo night. Amy used to sometimes accompany her mother until the rumors, or "whisper campaign" as her mama called it, had gotten out of hand. Thereafter Amy always felt a certain amount of guilt for messing up her mother's vice, the one thing that distracted her from her troubles with arthritis and the problems Amy had caused for her with her behavior.

This new vice wouldn't replace her present habit, but stacking another addiction on top of the other—this high brewed by the alchemy of fast money chased through a series of cash register clings and clangs, the tinkle of doubloons and the risk of watching it all drain away—would be a good buzz to add to the other one she already nursed. There was a chance that after she snuck off to the bathroom and did a line off the toilet's water tank that the two addictions being fed simultaneously would take her to the level of an exponentially new high.

"One-armed bandits are slot machines. You don't have to pull the lever on the side anymore." Aaron touched a silver handle attached to the side of a progressive jackpot machine. "Most of them are touchscreen. But I figure part of the fun for you would be cranking that arm. I mean, I don't think you're going to win much money, sweetheart."

"Can I smoke?"

Aaron looked over the tops of the slot machines, being tall enough to accomplish the task without having to reach up on his tiptoes. "Over there" he said, pointing right. "There's a smoking floor. You can play while you smoke over there."

"Great."

She'd had to cut back for his sake during the last three days, and she was itching for a cigarette, preferably something hard and mentholated, like a Newport One-Hundred in a box. She had spotted all manner of old timey tobacco shops and stands around the Res where various specialty cigarettes and plugs of chewing tobacco were kept in jars. The smell of meerschaum cherry tobacco was somehow pervasive all over the reservation, comingling with something Amy misidentified as aftershave, but was in fact the musky odor of treated parfleche leather.

"All right. I'm going back to the room to rest for awhile. Do you think you can handle yourself?"

Amy nodded.

"Remember. If they ask you for ID, give them the Jennifer license. It's the only one that looks like you, and the only one that will keep you legally in this room. You get locked up, I'm not bailing you out. Got it?"

"Uh-uh." She was already off in some corner of her own in her mind, already smoking her menthol cigarette, snorting the remaining eighth of Peruvian flake that she had left, already pulling that metal arm until coins appeared in the hopper like stars forming a magical constellation.

"Have fun," Aaron said as he turned. This would be the true test of her mettle. If she could stay out of trouble, not do something to double-cross him, well then maybe he would loosen the leash a little bit. Maybe he would even put some earnest effort into teaching her to drive, and he would let her use his truck to learn.

He passed an exercise room on his right, where a window gave him an unfortunate view of a Yuppie in gray spandex struggling upward on a

Stairmaster, his fat ass in Aaron's face, a ribbon of sweat pouring down the small of his back as he stared up into the battery of TVs turned to twenty-four hour cable news channels. The volume on the TVs was off and a black box that carried closed captions fought for space against both a stock ticker and another news crawl.

Aerobics never did it for him, but Aaron made a mental note to hit the weight pile later on, do some hammer curls until his biceps trembled beneath the flesh like baby skulls crowning from the womb, the ropy veins of his muscles coiling like testosterone-infused worms whose soil was tainted with anabolic steroids. He'd work in a couple of sets of squat thrust burnouts, some butterfly action for his shoulders and traps. He'd gotten into benching in the Corps and had once done competitive deadlifts, and had even placed second in a Joint Marines-ARVN jeep pull competition, wherein his CJ-3B-type had gotten stuck in the mud and the little Vietnamese bastard had beaten him over the line and won the case of Ba Moui Ba beer that was the prize.

Aaron slid the card in his door, sat down on the edge of the bed, and pulled the phone from his pocket. He hit "Contacts," entered "C," and selected "Chocoloate," which he had misspelled due to the trembling of his fingers as he entered the transsexual's phone information into his erotic Rolodex. It went directly to voicemail.

"Hi, this is your girl Chocolate, all woman with a little something extra. Pray for your girl to get the Adult Video News award for 'Best Solo Performance' this weekend, when I take the stage with Dynasty Rock to let the whole world—"

Aaron hung up and breathed deeply until the urge to put a hole in the wall subsided.

Amy went down the battery of machines, past the old woman with the bald patch who sat in her Rascal mobility scooter and fed quarters into a machine that promised perpetual jackpots and delivered nothing. She found her "one-armed bandit," as Aaron called it, a fitting cenotaph where she could pay respect to the woman who had given birth to her, but was now so far away. She felt like crying all of a sudden, but did not fear the impression she might make on anyone, as she was wearing the sunglasses Aaron had bought for her back in Nebraska and no one could see her eyes. They wouldn't notice her tears besides, she reasoned, as they were busy hemorrhaging their life savings away one coin at a time.

In front of her was a console whose cabinet featured artwork on one side showing airbrushed images of Bob Barker with his ionic white matching teeth and hair, his skin stretched tight and weathered like Tandoori chicken, an icepick-thin microphone in his left hand. On the other side of the machine was the First Lady of Game Shows herself, Miss Vanna White. It was some sort of "The Price is Right" and "Wheel of Fortune" combination machine. One of those shows, Amy couldn't remember which one, had always been her mother's favorite.

Amy inserted one of the few single dollars she had, determined to keep the Ben Franklin that Aaron had given her unbroken. She clicked the touchpad icon that spun the wheel. She prayed for money and hoped that the arrow didn't land on "Lose a Turn" or "Bankrupt."

Chapter Twelve

The parking lot of the gas station was well-lit and outside of the city, but something about it felt dangerous to the detective. The night air was crisp, with a sharpness that kept him on edge. The address of the BP matched the one on his pad that God gave him back at his apartment, and in a minute he was going to go inside and start asking some questions.

First, however, there was a call to make. He dialed Margaret Loeher, expecting her not to pick up. He liked to maintain something approximating daily contact with his clients, and he had missed her yesterday.

"Hello?" Her voice sounded gravelly.

"How are we holding up, Mrs. Loeher?"

"Detective, you forgot to finish cutting my yard the other day."

"I know. And now we've got another mystery on our hands."

"What's that?"

"We have to find out what happened to Mrs. Butterworth." Maggie Loeher blanked on the reference, and then seemed to recall it a moment later. She laughed, and her voice sounded hoarser than a moment before.

"Oh, the little gerbil. What was on that camera you found in the ground?"

"Maggie." He changed the subject, "It looks like Amy was involved with some bad people." He didn't want to tell the woman that her daughter had been hooking, but she would probably be able to read between the lines, he knew. "She was still pretty much around town long after you filed your missing persons on her. That means you were right about the cops not doing their job, unless Amy was wearing a really good disguise, but it doesn't seem probable to me that she was."

"I didn't mean to say that the cops hadn't tried at all. They did get my DNA on a national registry, you know like the one you see on Maury for the paternity suits?"

"Right." James thought for a moment that if Maggie Loeher watched the CSI/Law & Order "dead hooker" shows during her channel hopping odyssey, she no doubt came to expect too much of forensic science.

"They also took impressions of my teeth for... odomo?" She struggled for the word.

"Odontology?"

"Right, the cops did try."

"I understand. I just wanted to let you know that I am making progress and that—"

The gas station was directly in the flight path of a commercial airport and the banshee scream of jetliner engines roaring from takeoff made it impossible for Detective Arklow to hear either his own voice or Maggie's Loeher's response, and a moment later he lost signal and the call dropped. He glanced once at the face of his phone, and placed the cell in the coat pocket opposite his .38. Then he got out of his sedan and walked toward the front doors of the filling station.

He saw the night clerk through the glass, his fat form spilling around the sides of a Coors Silver Bullet neon sign that blinked above a red digital display showing the Power Ball jackpot had climbed to thirty million dollars. James held the door open for a small woman struggling with two large bags of ice, and then entered into the warm shop, coming in out of the night.

The clerk sat on a low vinyl stool, which all but disappeared beneath his egg-shaped girth. He had what James once heard uncharitably described as a "front butt," a massive overhang of fat at the midsection. The paunch was confrontational in its power, and projected forward like the figurehead on a ship. The mass of fat gave the man an androgynous look somehow at odds with his two-day stubble. He was pale, and had obviously been working nights for a long time, and had probably been comforting himself during those long stretches with whatever junk food was handy.

"How are you doing? I'm detective James Arklow."

The man looked down at a battery of security cameras housed on a monitor, and then looked back up at the detective. His mouth was slightly open. As he turned his head, James noticed he wore a Bluetooth. "You from the Health Department?"

"No, I'm investigating a missing person. I need to know what you do with the camera footage once you're done with it."

The door dinged, and a middle-aged woman wearing a leather Harley Davidson vest came in, nodded at the clerk, and walked toward the back. The clerk nodded back. James noted a nametag above the man's C-cup breasts, which said "Reggie".

Reggie said, "It used to be we had it on videocassette, in the old days. Now we have it burned on CD. We store it for a certain period of time and we then destroy it, unless it's needed."

"Why would you need it?"

"Oh, you know." Reggie shrugged, but his body was so heavy that it refused to oblige, and the shrugging motion ended with his neck. "If there's a robbery, maybe the GM thinks someone's stealing something."

Reggie excused himself, and James stood aside to let him ring up the woman biker's two Slim Jims and her pack of Pall Mall One-Hundreds in a soft pack. The clerk and customer bade each other goodnight, and Reggie turned his attention back to the detective.

"How long do you wait before throwing footage out?"

Another plane roared overhead, but its sound was thankfully muted inside the gas station. "A year."

"Great." James took his pad of paper out of his pocket. "I need to get a look at the footage for this day." He tore the sheet out and handed it to the clerk. The ballpark franks hummed as they rotated on the heated display case behind them.

"Okay." Reggie slowly lifted himself off his stool, and moved around the counter to the front of the store. He flipped the "Open" sign so that the "Closed" card faced the public, and he dimmed the "Open" neon next to the Silver Bullet ad. He locked the front door, and sifted through the keys on his chain. Then he looked at James and nodded. "Let's go."

He walked toward the back and opened the door. They entered into a little office crowded with papers scattered on every bit of shelf space. The walls were bare, save for a schedule that listed the cleaning rotation for employees, who was to clean the bathrooms when, and whose turn it was to take out the garbage. There was an ancient computer in the middle of the room balanced on a filing cabinet. It looked old enough to be a Commodore or a Tandy, and was open to a payroll screen.

"One more," Reggie said, walking to the back of the room and opening a second door. James followed him into the smaller room, which was its own miniature Big Brother nerve center, complete with a live feed split screen showing the front of the gas station, where a confused patron attempted to enter and got an unresponsive front door for all of their efforts.

There was a chair facing the TV monitor, which was the centerpiece in one massive long shelf where CDs in white paper sleeves were arranged like books on a library shelf.

Reggie ran his finger down along the rows, thumbing them with one hand while holding the piece of paper James Arklow had given him with the other. "September," he muttered quietly to himself. "Eighteenth... Eighteenth, eighteenth. Sixteen, seventeen, eighteen..."

He pulled the CD free of the shelf, and inserted it into the opening below the monitor screen in front of them. The monitor's picture switched from a live feed to grainy, recorded footage with the date and time stamp established in the lower left-hand corner. Reggie pulled the swivel chair out and held a hand toward James, inviting him to sit.

"Thanks," the detective said. "Listen, I'm going to be here probably for twenty-four hours, maybe more."

Whenever legwork required something especially onerous, like dumpster diving or *this*, it was his custom to remark that "This is why we get paid the big bucks." The line was always delivered sardonically, but as James muttered it under his breath now, the irony was especially rich considering that he was performing this case pro bono, merely to test his skills in order to satisfy for himself the question of whether or not he still had 'it,' the ephemeral, intangible quality required to crack cases. There was also, in the back of his mind, the very selfish desire to solve this case in such a way that the resolution would prove irresistible to the editors of *Private Investigators Monthly*. Hell, he told himself, he might even make the cover.

He did not feel especially lucky at the moment, though, and in fact felt only somewhat tired. Reggie, accommodating host that he was, seemed to appreciate the gravity of the task the detective had ahead of him, a consanguine bond established perhaps when he remembered that rare triple shift he was forced worked oh so many nights ago.

"I'll get you some coffee," he said.

"Thanks," James replied, truly grateful. He cracked his knuckles, did a couple of neck rolls, and watched the monitor. It was 12:02 a.m. onscreen. The black and white footage showed two teenagers with hooded sweatshirts stealing Hostess treats in the center aisle of the store, stuffing the snack cakes into the single pockets of their zip-up hoodies. Outside, a big rig was filling up one of its two one-hundred and fifty gallon tanks with diesel, and on the side of the building, a homeless man was discreetly urinating on a wall while a cat watched him. It was not exactly *Masterpiece Theater*.

Chapter Thirteen

It was useless to try to comprehend how the two of them had gone from such tranquility a few hours ago to such tension right now. The plan had been to spend the day and the rest of the evening at the Wind River Hotel, gambling the afternoon away and slumbering the rest of the night in the comparative luxury of their handicapped bedroom. Now, however, Aaron Neblett and Amy Loeher were on the road again. The truck was pointed south, on a trajectory toward an abyss blacker than the inescapable darkness which had been gathering quietly around them since they made their deal in that basement. They felt it, but neither of them spoke.

They were at the southern edge of the reservation, in a patch of Wyoming that was bleak at the height of day, and far more ominous at night. The skeletal outlines of derelict, abandoned oil works rose from the destabilized vestiges of sand dunes collapsing around them on either side of the road. There was very little manmade light present, but the moon was high and bright enough to shine down on the ugly rock formations just beyond the sand dunes in the near-distance, one outcropping shaped like a poisonous mushroom, another forming banded columns that resembled a massive Sienna skirt, which could have belonged to a ghostly giantess now dancing her dark fandango without a partner under the starry skies.

They were far from the pollution of the city, and the constellations announced themselves one to the other in the black saucer above them. Aaron Neblett shook his head and looked over at the girl. He finally spoke. "That was a dumb move you pulled, little bitch."

"I'm sorry."

She wanted things to go back to where they had been earlier today. She stifled tears, ran over the preceding hours in her mind, trying to find out exactly where and how she had ruined an otherwise eventless afternoon.

First, he had given her the one-hundred dollar bill and left her to do her thing at the slot machines. He'd given her a couple of admonitions and some final parting advice, and then headed off to the room. What he had neglected to tell her, however, was how fast she would burn through that hundred by pulling the metal arm on the side of that slot machine and praying for that "Jackpot" adorned with a spangled dollar sign that tempted her, filled either of her irises and came to function as some sort of brass ring that had to be clutched, that, once held, would solve all of her life's problems.

Amy Loeher had fed all one-hundred of her single dollar bills into the machine. After two hours of gaming, she glanced away from the machine, blinking her eyes as they stung and she struggled to adjust to the darkness of the casino pit. She looked around the lobby and saw a man with an ostrich feather in his porkpie hat, clutching his lucky rabbit foot in one hand and a cupful of quarters in the other. There was also a woman with elephantine legs, where the calves and the ankles merged, chasing her phantom fruit across a touchscreen that was not paying out. Seeing that made Amy come crashing back to reality, realizing that a bump of coke could solve some of her problems, but that there was a deeper sting, something about her mother dogging her, eating her up inside. She knew that heading back to the hotel room at that point was not an option, that Aaron would not have been happy to see her, and that they both truly needed a break from one another after the last few hours together on the road, and before the next few that would carry them on into Sacramento.

In an effort to avoid annoying Aaron she decided to wander the floor and kill some time. Having just suffered financial slaughter at the jackpots, she fled from that battery of ugly robotic monsters onto the floor, where the cardsharps matched their skills against each other, and in the pits against dealers and croupiers. It was a more comfortable environment, even if Aaron had been right about her inability to understand the games.

She drifted from craps to roulette, over to the blackjack table, finally coming to rest at a poker game where a stack of burgundy chips adjacent to another tower of pumpkin-colored chips caught her eye. Amy didn't know one denomination from another, but she knew enough to know that the two thuggish gentlemen going against the house dealer were both high rollers, and the hustler inside of her came alive.

God had pimped her out on gambling junkets before in Vegas, and they had been a nightmarish whir of golfers in Lacoste shirts taking out their erectile dysfunction on her in their cars, and Japanese businessmen secluded in their penthouse suites struggling to convey unspeakable demands to her in broken English.

Amy hadn't spotted any other working girls swimming on the stroll, unless they were being very covert about it. As she walked the halls, from table to table, she sensed the gathering worshipful attention of eyes. She felt the power her youth, beauty, and above all her white skin had on the men who watched her as she passed. She thought of how God called her his "little snow bunny" during his more affectionate moments, played her off against the darker girls in his stable by explaining within their earshot that white girls were more marketable with big-spending Arabs and other international clientele.

She walked the floor with God's words ringing in her ears, and knew that as long as the attention of the men lasted, the mileage on her body and the abuse she had been dealt meant nothing. She was fresh, clean, vindicated by their desire, and the men were beneath her. The truth, ultimately, was that however much she told herself that she needed a break from hoeing, however put out or exasperated she felt with the ceaseless constant attention, the innuendo, the flirting both invited and unsolicited, she needed it all as much as she hated it. And the second the money ran out at the slot machine, she was looking for a man who would look at her, who would watch her, who would give her attention.

Amy found two such men at that table. The first one had a progression of three teardrops tattooed beneath his left eye, beginning at the height of his cheekbone and ending at his upper jaw. His head was shaved, and there was a massive scar bisecting his broad scalp. His partner was just as bald, and twice as fat, though without tattoos or scars. His choice of hairstyle was especially unfortunate for him, however, since the back of his head was one deformed mass of Shar Pei folds, truncating in ridges of fat which resembled a pack of franks gathering on the back of his neck.

Once Amy eavesdropped long enough to match the color of the chips with their value, she did the math between small talk and cadging for drinks, and figured that the boys had fifty thousand or so dollars at play on the table, and that their only reaction to five grand lost on a hand was to order another round of Mojitos and laugh about their change in luck.

Amy's initial plan was to charge them for a double, one-thousand dollars for them to make a sadistic rotisserie of her body, with some possible race play and an uglier than normal character to their routine, since she was white and her body might be the vessel for their revenge. She had been there many times with black men in group settings, and also knew from experience that one-on-one the darker submissive secrets came out, the hushed request to be called a slave or to drop the n-bomb. She would have braced herself for the contingency of playing master, slave, or doing straight missionary, provided they were willing to front her a thousand up front for the deed.

The game plan changed however, after the boys experienced a run of luck and built their stake to $75,000. She told them her name was Jennifer, and showed them her ID. The skinnier, tattooed thug told her his name was Bad Feather, and that his cousin's name was Johnny Little Sky. They moved on to their fourth round of Mojitos, while Amy deliberately nursed her first drink as slowly as possible.

She planned to ask them if they wanted her to come back to their room, but what came out when she next spoke was, "Do you guys want to buy some Yay?"

The two Arapahoe cousins exchanged a look at that point, tapered their play at the table, and bowed out after nearly breaking even on their fifty-grand grubstake.

"How much?" Bad Feather asked.

"Five ounces…" She sounded certain when she said it, but knew she was winging it. Aaron might not go in for selling any dope, but she didn't want to fuck, or get fucked by any men at the moment. She wanted their desire, and their money, but she did not want to be used, not with the weight of her mother's worry and arthritis and her own humiliation pounding in her head as her name rang out through the church pews she envisioned in her mind, not with all of that crashing in on her at the moment. No, she wanted to fuck them over.

"What do you want for five O's?" Johnny Little Sky asked, clutching his cousin around the neck drunkenly with the hand he used to hold his empty Mojito glass, his grip so unsteady that the maraschino-draped parasol threatened to fall free of his iced cup onto the carpet florid with peacocks.

"One large," Amy said. "And I'll suck both y'all dicks when we're done."

They didn't bother to suppress their smiles at that point, wide and ugly, all but telepathically communicating with their eyes that the girl would be easy to push over, to brace for whatever cocaine she had and whatever they wanted to take from her body. She wanted them to believe in her helplessness, and knew it was worth whatever anger Aaron Neblett might throw her way when he got involved, and she was responsible for the harm he caused to the men who wanted to use her body.

They exchanged phone numbers there at the card table, gathered in a conspiratorial huddle the dealer had the good sense not to break. Amy then headed back to the hotel room, greeting Aaron cheerfully, making him happy for the time being. He was on the edge of the king-sized bed, his heavy boots off and the dirty bottoms of his socks pointed toward an old episode of M*A*S*H playing on the TV screen.

The curtains were drawn wide open, and after doing a line, Amy asked Aaron, "Do you ever golf?" She admired the oceans of furrowed and combed green rollicking just beyond their window's edge.

"Nah," Aaron said, twirling the remote. "I know a guy hauls reefers for Nebraska Meats, though, he makes it a point to stop at all the public courses when he's driving a load."

"Reefers?" Amy asked, daubing her fingertips below her nostrils, checking for blood. "You mean, like weed? Marijuana?"

"That's a good one. I mean reefers, like refrigerated vans."

"Oh."

That had been the end of their conversation, and Amy had been afraid that she would not be able to breach the subject of the two Arapahoe kinfolk, that Aaron would fly off the handle and maybe kill her if she told him she had informed two strange men that she was carrying coke, or that she had set up a deal without informing the rightful owner of the aforementioned dope.

She decided to save the details for dinner. That way if she sprung it on him and he got angry,

Aaron Neblett would at least be forced to delay the project of killing her until after they ate and were no longer in public. The lone Anglo on the wait staff took their order, a chipper blonde kid who wore an arrowhead bolo tie.

"We'll both have the twelve ounce New York strips, with the rock lobster tails," Aaron said, gathering both of their menu placards in his hand and passing them to the waiter.

"And I'll also have the vanilla-bean extract Cream Brule for desert," Amy said.

If the waiter thought her mispronunciation of "Crème Brule" was humorous, he stifled his amusement as he took their menus and departed. She looked at Aaron who was spread out in his booth, taking his full ease across the entire length of the vinyl upholstery. For the first time ever, she saw him without his full uniform of company hat, patched jacket, and tinted prescription specs. He was an unattractive weather-beaten scarecrow of a man, a gaunt yet muscled monster, but for all of that he seemed peaceful, a predator luxuriating in the lull between mealtimes on the asphalt Serengeti.

She hated to spoil the aura of relaxation he was cultivating, but she knew this was the time to tell Aaron what she had done.

"I ran into a couple of Indian dudes who want to buy a few ounces of blow off you."

He listened, and drummed his fingers on the tabletop, and so she kept speaking. "I figure we could split the profits fifty-fifty."

Aaron Neblett continued to drum his fingers, making little syncopated paradiddle patterns with his tarantula-like hands, cracking rim shots and high hat snaps with the index and middle digits, in counterpoint to the Muzak weakly piped in through overhead speakers. An appetizer of dinner rolls came a moment later, and Aaron remained quiet throughout the rest of the repast.

Afterwards they went up to the hotel room, where he took a long, hot shower, and Amy watched a TV show about teenage witches that had her fantasizing about what it would be like to possess magical powers.

Aaron emerged from the bathroom thirty minutes later, fully dressed and wearing a determined expression on his face. "Tell them okay. Tell them to meet us in the parking lot. Tell them what my rig looks like."

He dragged her out of the room shortly thereafter. He checked out of the hotel, turning in their keycards and agreeing to pay the full price for the night without making any kind of protest. He left without explaining anything to Amy, who was too frightened and confused to form words as he led her across the lobby, out of the Wind River Hotel and Casino and into the truck. He got into the driver's seat and Amy climbed in on the passenger's side. Aaron told her to call the two brothers and she did.

The two Arapahos, Bad Feather and Johnny, showed up in the parking lot behind them twenty minutes later, flashing the custom fog lights on their gunmetal I-Roc Z Camaro in order to gain their attention. Aaron squinted as the bright light filled his convex mirrors. His hat was on, pulled low over his forehead, and he put his shades on to complete the transformation. The change left no doubt in Amy's mind. They were no longer on vacation.

Aaron then started the truck, giving the diesel engine some time to wake up, revving it and watching the tachometer and voltage readout, glancing from one indicator to another, checking fluid levels, watching left, right, and above like a conductor supervising his supplicating pit orchestra.

"Call them again," Aaron said, "And tell them to follow us for a spell."

He pulled out of the parking lot, driving in the direction of the stars waking on the frosted northern horizon. Amy hadn't expected them to be gullible enough to fall for it, but they were drunk, and swerved along the road behind Aaron's rig.

They had been following him for some time now, and Amy remained silent during the hairpin turns, and through the switchback trails hugging the sheer-faced buttes. She kept quiet and contrite. When Aaron next spoke, there was something in his tone that made her wonder if he had forgiven her. She saw a smile creep across his face, and she knew then that there was nothing to forgive, that he had never really been angry and that he was as glad for this opportunity as she was.

"All right," he said, "When we pull over, I want you to fire this into the sky." He reached under his seat and handed her a flare pistol. It held one twelve-gauge shell in its revolving body.

Amy took it in her hand, surprised by its weight. God had guns, but she had never touched one before, even one of this low variety. She felt the power inherent in its weighty metal contours. She knew that she was not innocent, knew that she would be an accomplice, and she reminded herself again that this was what she wanted.

"Where should I fire it?"

"Doesn't matter," Aaron said. "As long you don't fire it in the cab." He laughed. "Fire up into the sky, fire directly at one of them sons of bitches. Light his head up like a jack-o-lantern for all I care." He laughed again, and this time Amy laughed with him.

The cab lurched as Aaron downshifted and the Jake brake shuddered. To their right there was a yellow diamond-shape roadside sign whose symbol was hard to misinterpret even in this half-light. Below the crude blocky image of a rig, the sign said: "Runaway Trucks."

"This is a good spot," Aaron said, and steered right. The silver Camaro behind them followed closely on their bumper.

The two-car convoy pulled forward into a canyon, a sylvan pocket in the otherwise arid country of rocks and sand. Several trees were bent in torturous shapes, having been subjected to relentless high winds that perverted them into agonized parodies. Stranger still was that these stunted trees shared real estate with others of equal size which grew straight, as they were shielded by mammoth sandstone boulders which protected them from the wind, allowing them to grow to mightier heights.

Aaron aimed the cab for the deep sands of the muddy pit just beyond the slowly-graded ramp directly in front of them. He pulled to a stop, killed the lights, and engaged the brake, sending a shivering serpentine hiss through the truck as he completed the stop. The Camaro growled behind them and then grew still. Its lights dimmed a moment later.

"All right," Aaron said. "When you get out, hit it." Amy looked at him. She saw the Taurus revolver shining in his hand.

"Okay."

Aaron dropped down from the truck, walked around the side, toward the back of the cab. Two competing drunken voices shouted toward the cloud-swept saucer of a moonlit sky spread like a white lattice above them. "Shit, man, I got to take a piss. I got ten mixed drinks running through my Johnson."

"I know, right?"

The fatter one faced a giant petrified sequoia, struggling to brace himself against the tree with one hand while holding his penis with the other. Aaron pointed the pistol, steadied the crosshairs where the man's brainstem joined the neck. He squeezed the trigger, and the report of his shot was muffled in the phosphorous hiss of a bright flare whose pyrotechnic striation drew the eye of the skinnier Arapahoe brother, who let out an appreciative "Ooh!" as if he was enjoying a fireworks display.

His cousin was wrapped in a pile of bloodied pine needles and twigs broken off from a sapling nearby. Aaron pivoted around the back of the truck and faced the tattooed red man dressed in a powder blue football jersey. The man's eyes reflected the knowledge of his impending death for a period of time too finite to be counted, but which was felt by both him and his killer, and expanded into something larger than eternity as he watched Aaron's eyes and Aaron watched his, the last three bullets shedding their brass jackets and eating into his organ meat without thought or pity.

Tissue, deep and black, flew out of the skinny drunken Arapaho's back. He slid on his battered coccyx across the syrupy bed of pine needles, and slammed back first into the hollow base of a tall Engelmann spruce. The tree gathered him into its dark trunk. Aaron brushed the coil of cordite-smelling smoke away from his face, waved his gun like a hot potato for thirty seconds or so, and coughed. Amy came around from the passenger side of the truck, shock and ecstasy moving across her face in lambent shades, with ecstasy winning out a moment later.

"I killed them," Amy said. "I killed those men."

"Not really. I kind of killed them. You did a good job distracting that joker, though."

He put his Taurus revolver in the inside pocket of his satin jacket, took the flare gun from Amy's limp grasp. He walked over to the dead fat man, ran his hands through his pockets. Aaron discarded the man's keys, condoms, and wallet into a bed of pine needles beside the body.

"Shit." He turned toward Amy. "Go through that redskin's pockets. See if you can't find those ducats."

"Huh?" Amy's nose and forehead creased in a hopeless attempt to join into one confused mass of pale flesh.

"The money! See if he's got the dough on him."

The new moon provided more than enough light to work by, and he was losing patience.

"What about…" Amy faltered, standing over the corpse, her previous excitement dissipated. She had wanted a man destroyed, crushed before her, but not like this, not really dead. She wondered how much of the blame was hers, how much of the murder (or murders, since there were two dead bodies out here) was her doing. No doubt both men were subpar specimens of humanity. Both may have come out here with the intent of raping her on their minds, possibly burning Aaron for his dope in a double-cross, or maybe they were just too drunk to think straight and formulate a plan of any kind. Something about it all felt wrong to her, though. She had crossed some kind of threshold, she knew, and was now in league with the trucker.

"What about what?" Aaron flipped the fat body and went over to the Camaro.

"What about fingerprints? Shouldn't I wear gloves?"

"Yeah, and I'll tell you what. Why don't you get that surveillance footage out of that CCTV they keep mounted in that big redwood tree over there." He shook his head in the dark. "Jesus Christ, no wonder I found you tricking as a lot lizard. Selling your derriere is about the only profession you're cut out for."

Aaron opened both the driver's and passenger's doors on the car. He hit the cabin light switch, searching in the glowing interior for the money. He felt along the dashboard, checked the cup holder and the mats in the floorboards. He cussed, muttered against God under his breath and flipped the glove compartment open.

"Ah!"

"What?" Amy asked.

He killed the lights in the silver Camaro and emerged from the car with a Ziploc-sealed package of one hundred dollar bills. He unzipped the bag, broke the seal, and took a deep whiff of the money, the potent scent of ink and paper filling his lungs, the freshness of it like the renewing smell that assaults one upon entering a used bookstore or riding for the first time in a clean rental car. He exhaled dramatically, pleased with himself and the world.

“I need a bump,” Amy said. She was almost finished with the second bag, and would honestly have zero qualms about asking Aaron for another. She had earned it, paid whatever kind of penance she owed, and not even he could deny it, she knew. He seemed to defer, nodding in a conspiratorial manner as he removed the chain from around his neck and threw it to her.

“Not yet, sweetheart. First, grab Uncle Aaron that axe in the headache rack. It should be next to the First Aid kit and the safety warning cones.”

“Yes sir,” she said, wondering to herself as she caught the key whether or not she intended to be sarcastic with her deference to him, or if she was willing to bend that far on his behalf. Usually, she had some leverage on men. Even God treated her royally on occasion because she was his “snow bunny,” his ever marketable white princess. She had to admit that she liked this better. She was useful for something besides sex, for once.

She ran over to the truck and hopped up, sidestepping the pigtail, the coiled lines, and other color-coded hardware that she didn’t understand. She inserted the key into the headache rack, and slowly lowered the face of the cab-guard case. Inside were various road-related paraphernalia held in Velcro sleeves, racked and waiting to be put to good use. Here was a grease gun, there a Maglite.

“Hurry up!” Aaron shouted, but his voice was more playful than severe.

Amy saw the axe situated next to the First Aid kit, which was snapped shut. She glanced backwards once, saw Aaron counting the stack of cash he had removed from the plastic bag, and then she looked back to the little tin white case. It was not much larger than a lunchbox. She wondered as she quietly snapped it open how far into her addiction she was, how far into the more vaguely defined concept of "the life" she was since she now found herself disobeying a man who had just readied two souls for eternity. Why, she asked herself, am I opening this case up, sneaking out a condom not much larger than a breakfast blintz, from among the...she counted them...fifteen remaining condoms, when I know this can get me killed?

She did not proffer an answer because she was scared of it, scared of herself, and so she instead slid the condom down between her sweating breasts which hung loose in the bra that clung tightly to her sundress, with its myriad butterflies and their gorgeous prisms of exploding colors. She tried to shoo thoughts of the two men she had just killed (or helped kill) away with the fantasy she conjured in her mind. The two Arapahoe boys she lured out here were now to find their eternal resting place in a blissful field of purple poppies, lorded over by a fluttering army of radiant and joyful butterflies, monarchs flapping above the men's graves and filling their nostrils and eye sockets with golden light. It was nonsense dredged spontaneously, she knew, but it made her feel better.

Amy Loeher closed the face of the First Aid kit, grabbed the axe from its Velcro sleeve, and ran back over to Aaron. In the time she had been gone, he had made a functional workbench from the hood of the I-Roc classic, and there were two piles of cash, stacked side by side, crisp and green, above the left high beam.

"Which one's mine?" Amy realized that sounded forward, but she wanted her cut, if only because after they were finished divvying, she knew she could go toot in the sleeper berth of the truck.

"They're both ten large. Knock yourself out."

She would have to be careful, make sure to ask him for another bag soon. If she just kept her mouth shut and dipped into the next bag, he would begin to suspect that she had stolen one. If she asked for another one either later today or tomorrow, he might bitch that she was snorting too fast, but he would not be especially vicious. And there was ultimately only one way to find out if he knew for sure exactly how many bags there were in the headache rack, and whether or not he knew she had stolen any from him. She would have to send him back there to get another one.

"Thanks," Amy said. She had seen more money in her previous life, much more in fact when it was tax season at Casa de God, but this was the first time she had seized so much in her hand at one time for purposes other than counting out God Body Divine's haul for the day. It would have taken at least fifty men to net her what now filled her hand, she knew, the same number it had taken to widen her vagina from the size of a bottleneck to a pharmaceutical bottle, and then to...she didn't want to think about the wear and tear.

It was hard to maintain any particular train of thought at the moment, anyway. She wanted to know what Aaron was going to do with the axe. She got her answer a moment later. He walked over to the body of the skinny tattooed gangster sprawled and limp beneath the spruce tree. He dragged the body out in front of the Camaro, spread it so that the limbs were splayed evenly apart. He lifted the axe high and dropped it on the dead man's knee, disarticulating bone, flesh, and cartilage in one odd crunching sound which could not have been mistaken for anything other than what it was.

"Oh, God!" Amy shouted.

"Look the other way if you can't handle it."

She turned to the tree line where the moon shone. The sound was still there, though, a crunch that now sounded like a stale loaf of French bread being torn by hand, cracking as it yielded. Aaron spoke as he heaved from the exertion. "After I get the arms and heads off, I'll drag those and the torsos over to the sandpit. No one will come looking. You just watch the road and let me know if you see any trucks headed for the runaway ramp, okay?"

Amy could not respond. She was vomiting.

Chapter Fourteen

Something strange happened at 1:43 a.m. on the surveillance video, which was 11:47 p.m. according to Detective James Arklow's wristwatch. After roughly an hour and a half of dull security footage, people pumping gas and washing their windows, three semi rigs pulled over to the right side of the gas station and disappeared from view.

James was just about to get out of his chair and head to the front of the store to get Reggie, when the clerk returned with a fresh refill of coffee. "Thank you," Detective Arklow said, accepting his Styrofoam cup with one hand, carefully balancing the hot coffee, and pointing at the screen with his other.

"Some trucks just disappeared around back of the station. What are they doing back there?"

"Oh." Reggie leaned over the detective's shoulder. "They're parking for a couple of hours, getting some shuteye. A lot of over-the-road truckers use their TA frequent fueler cards here. They've got rules about how many hours they can drive. A lot of them have dispatchers who keep track of how long they've been going. If they don't stop every once and awhile, they can get fined by the Department of Transportation."

"How do you know all of this?"

Reggie picked an undefined bit of crust from the edge of his nose. "How does the waitress at the diner learn so much about cops? She serves them coffee and listens to them chat. I've got all the time in the world to eavesdrop."

He looked toward the front of the store. Another clerk had shown up sometime after midnight, but Reggie still seemed eager to get back to the front and tend the counter. However James still had another question or two in reserve. "You ever run across any weird truckers?"

"Yeah. Most of them are weird." He picked his nose again, this time less discreetly. Then he pointed with the offending finger at the screen from which James had momentarily taken his eyes. "Truth of the matter is that a lot of truckers have another reason for putting it in park."

"What do you mean?" James had an idea, but he wanted to hear it from the clerk.

"Oh, they're not just here for the free Wi-Fi hotspots, if you get my drift."

The clerk's innuendo was given a visual aid a moment later, the detective's question answered as two girls, one white and one black, sauntered into view. The black girl was an ebony bombshell, her curves lending credence to the theory of life's origins dawning on the fertile Sub-Saharan plains of Africa. She wore a shiny one piece outfit splashed with a pattern borrowed from the American flag, stars exploding beneath the mounds of her Nubian breasts, her ass straining as if overinflated and almost buoyant enough to tear the seat of her dress.

The white girl behind her balanced herself precariously on a pair of clear jelly heels, her micro skirt green and frilled at the hemline like a Hawaiian lei. The black girl disappeared from view as the seconds ticked away. The white girl was Amy Loeher.

He shot forward in his seat, and dropped his scalding hot coffee on the floor. “Hey, watch it!” The hot cup of black Joe spilled across the sticky tiles, and Reggie backed up two or three paces to escape the steaming puddle as it formed. “Jesus, man.”

James ignored him, and paid the graveyard shift clerk no heed as the man cursed and stomped out of the room. He watched Amy disappear after the black girl on the screen. The minutes passed on the time stamp displayed in the lower left-hand corner. Then there was the creaky sound of ungreased wheels squeaking across the greasy floor behind him. James could hear Reggie sloshing water into a mop bucket, and he could smell the minty putrid scent of some industrial-grade cleaning solvent mixed with hot water. It hissed, and James imagined that the chemical was green.

“You should be more careful,” Reggie said.

“Shush.”

“What?”

“Shut up for a minute,” James said, tuning out Reggie, standing as he saw the rig half jackknife from left to right as it struggled into view, as the little corn blonde girl with the tropical micro skirt and the clear heels fought in the cab with the man whose outline James could only vaguely make out. The cab pulled forward and disappeared. The black prostitute struggled in the wake of the truck's flight out of the parking lot, coughing as she ran through a cloud of carbon monoxide, lost a heel, retrieved the same, and threw it at the retreating form of the rig which sped off with her partner in tow.

"That's it!" James shouted.

"What?" Reggie released the mop from the ringer and let go of the handle.

"Rewind it!" James shouted. "Where is the controller?!"

"Oh, here you go." He took a small, black plastic remote from on top of a metal filing cabinet and handed it to James, who all but snatched the control out of the night cashier's hand. Reggie moved until he stood behind the detective and watched, remaining silent.

"Come on," James said. He hit "Rewind," all but mashed the button with his thumb, as the black girl danced backwards, retrieved her shoe, drew in a breath of carbon exhaust, and disappeared from the screen, making way to accommodate the truck's body, at least sixty-plus feet of tractor, emblazoned with a red emblem which was large enough to make pausing all but unnecessary. James froze the frame anyway. He was so excited by the break in the case that he accidentally went into the left pocket of his camelhair coat, putting his hand on the butt of the air-weight .38 when he had intended to grab his pencil and pad. His false start for the gun made Reggie's eyes shift nervously.

He seized the pencil stub in his hand, flipped to an open page, and wrote: "Nebraska Meats."

"Got your ass," he said, and set the pad and paper on top of the desk where he sat. He then pressed "Rewind" again, pulling the tractor backwards into the night and off-camera, putting the cab of the truck directly in his line of sight before he hit pause again. "All right."

Reggie watched James as he made shorthand notes in the paltry margins of his little booklet, things about hair, weight, and age. On screen, all Reggie saw were two bodies thrashing in the cab, blotting out the window and filling the camera's eye with their flurrying, blurred shapes. One was a woman, the other a man, and not much else was evident to the clerk from this angle.

The detective finished writing and hit "Rewind" again, thinking back to the dull early opening salvo of this voyeuristic stakeout, when he was forced to watch one customer after another queue up to the less than photogenic Reggie, who handed them scratch-off lottery tickets, cigarettes, beer, and other false forms of hope before taking their money and handing them their change. Among that long line of waiting bodies, shuffling in and out of the glare of the fluorescent light, underneath the gaze of the cameras, buttressed by the fisheye convex mirrors at the back of the store designed to discourage shoplifting, James searched for someone who matched the vague form he had spotted and taken note of struggling with Amy Loeher in the truck cab during those few frames he had to work from.

Reggie got restless behind him, as the wet coffee-stained floor dried. James finally saw who he was looking for, and when he hit pause this time, he noted all of the details at his leisure. There was no young and terrified blond to strafe and flail around and unintentionally obstruct the detective's view in this rare frozen frame. There was no annoying reflection, the glare of light reflecting off the Windex-streaked window of the cab pulling off in a cloud of exhaust. There was now only a picture fit for a framed 8 x 10 glossy, a snapshot of a man who stood well north of six feet, wore a satin company jacket with enough patches to give the impression that he won every spelling bee since the sixth grade, and kept a beard and a matching shoulder-length mane of hair worthy of Sampson but more befitting a lumberjack. His features were buried underneath a tacky mesh trucker hat with an adjustable strap and a cardboard flat bill.

He wore sunglasses, but James couldn't tell whether they were prescription, or maybe he was just the kind of asshole who chose to wear them inside at night. The man bought some beef jerky from Reggie the night clerk and then disappeared from the camera's view.

James searched the remote for the "Stop" button. He hit it, and he spun toward Reggie. "I'm going to need a copy of that tape. I'll definitely have to use it in court if we catch this son of a bitch."

"Keep it," Reggie said, reaching over the detective, ejecting the CD, and placing it back in its white sleeve.

"Won't your boss notice if it's missing?" James asked, standing.

"A bunch of them are missing, thanks to that same boss, matter of fact."

"What do you mean?"

"I mean, if he sees something out of the ordinary that he finds funny, like a fight or something like that, he keeps it. One time a guy was smoking at the pump and he set his arm on fire. Another time, this guy came in off the road, asleep at the wheel of his VW, and he frigging plowed through the front of the store. He shattered the glass. He hit a pyramid display of Bud Light. It was frigging awesome."

"Thanks." Detective Arklow waved the CD in its white paper case. "I mean it." He walked around the cashier, stepped gingerly over the wet spot where the man previously mopped.

"It's cool." Reggie followed him out toward the front of the gas station. "Bill thinks he's going to send in that crash to "World's Worst Work-

Related Accidents" and that's going to put us on the map."

"Bill?"

"The GM, the General Manager."

"Right." James walked to the front door, opened it as a frigid gust poured inside. A tiny Cessna flashed its underbelly at him as it descended toward a landing strip somewhere out there in the darkness. He hopped into his car and started the engine. The glow-in-the-dark clock on his dashboard said 2:24 a.m. He had never heard of Nebraska Meats, but he took the name of the firm at face value and expected that when he looked them up, he would find their address listed somewhere in Nebraska. It was almost a certainty that they didn't open until 9 a.m. That left him with some time to kill.

The moon above was pure and white. The bright power of the frostbitten orb made him shiver as he beheld it, even with the benefit of the heat on high and the windows of his sedan rolled up. He pulled out and drove, the anonymous features of the little highway exit town interchangeable with those of any one found at a given off-ramp in each of the fifty states. People lived here, he reminded himself as he drove. The motels were multistoried purgatories where the cable TV shows and the vending machine fare made the nights too bland for dreaming, and the gas stations were bright havens where the third shift employees basked in the midnight fluorescence like lizards sunning themselves on gray rocks. The detective felt his eyes growing heavy, and knew that if he let himself go to sleep he might wake up too late to call Nebraska Meats first thing in the morning.

He decided to stop at the first diner he saw, and turned into a café with the very utilitarian name of "Restaurant," whose sign was made even plainer by the dimmed neon of the first "R" in its title. It was "Estaurant," or nothing, however, at this late hour. James parked and walked through the front door, and seated himself as the sign posted next to the hostess's stand instructed him to do.

The walls of the restaurant were knotty pine, adorned with group photos of the local little league team, sporting their jerseys and gathered on benches in dugouts. There was also a small trophy case, filled with miniature Heisman statues and Stanley Cups. It took five minutes for James to figure out that the buffet was the only option available this late (or this early). He helped himself to two boiled eggs skewered with toothpicks, as well as half a rack of ribs he rived away from a whole rack that dripped with translucent flesh, using a pair of salad tongs to extricate the baby back morsels.

He ate quickly, and didn't need to wait until he finished to feel the first pangs of indigestion, the bilious protest of a stomach that knew it was too old to take this much stress, coffee, red meat, and hours without sleep. Teaching courses at the university had pampered him, and throwing himself into this investigation had forced his circadian rhythms more out of whack than crossing three time zones on a nonstop flight across the country. When a waitress with a high piled bouffant by the name of Janine finally came by with a pitcher of black coffee, he drank and thought he could sense the black acrid Joe leaking through what felt like the perforated ulcer in his stomach that Amy Loeher had worn into his gut over the last few days.

He put away three cups of coffee. He drank until his fingers shook like dragonfly wings and he was forced to grip the ersatz porcelain contours of his coffee mug just to keep his cup from spilling. Classic country played over the loudspeakers, the plaintive yarn of Lefty Frizzell and his "Long Black Veil," seguing into the maudlin heartbreak of Marty Robbins, wailing his sad tale of unrequited love, until the classic country songs ended with Charley Pride's "Kiss an Angel Good Morning," and became cowboy music. Merle Haggard was carefully delineating what the folks did and didn't do in Muskogee, and then the outlaws Johnny Paycheck and Johnny Cash sang about Chillicothe Penitentiary and Folsom Prison, respectively.

It was the kind of restaurant where James was not surprised to get change on a ten dollar bill, and the short order cook might have to take a five minute break from slinging hash to talk with his parole officer by the dumpster out back for a spell. The moon eventually traded places with the sun, whose bright light significantly dampened the charms of Estaraunt and threw the establishment into a chiaroscuro grimy enough to warrant a few handwritten "Wash Me" signs in the bay window fronting the street.

The detective left the change the waitress had given him on the table, walked back out to his car, and drove to the Extended Stay. His laptop was open, hibernating among the comforter and sheets scattered on top of his bed, right where he left it. He gave the track pad of his laptop an imperceptible brush with his finger and did a Google search for "Nebraska Meats." The first website's information stated, "Nebraska Meats provides organic, farm fresh Bison, both in patties and ground form, to customers as far away as—"

James clicked the link, ignored all of the promotional boilerplate, felt the old excitement when the logo at the top of the webpage was the same one he had seen on that truck wherein Amy had been struggling with the driver in the cab. Their hours were listed as "9 a.m.-4 p.m. Monday-Friday" and their telephone number and address, in the heart of Downtown North Platte, Nebraska, were listed on the page as well. James entered the telephone number into his cellphone, knowing that he would only have to press the little phone-shaped icon once to be connected.

If he were to call the place right now, however, it would no doubt go directly to voicemail. The digital clock on the cable box above his TV said

6:43 am. A little bit more than two hours to go, he told himself, and then he sprawled out on the massive bed. The idiot box was still muted, turned to The Weather Channel. A massive cloud front was amassing in the Delta region, giving the porcine meteorologist in his shiny polyester suit much cause to gesticulate and frame the coming storm with his meaty hands.

Thoughts came to James unbidden, bringing with them an equally unwanted erection. He thought of one of his undergrads, Emily Watterson, a graceful and silent creature, powder pale with full dark lips. She had the insolent habit of starting a question before her hand was raised, and following one query up with a battery of further questions if she felt so inclined, grinding the entire class to a halt. Her legs were usually bare, glossed to a high shine and giving off an aloe scent which was hard to ignore. Professor Arklow would sometimes find himself caught off-guard by the sight of them, the different contours revealed with each of the various ways that she managed to cross or fold them. A slight panic would go through him when he saw them, something probably similar to what dramatic performers felt when they saw a hostile, mocking set of eyes in the crowd.

The beauty of her legs was like most things illicit, something he would have preferred to drink in at his leisure, and was in reality forced to glance at in passing, stealing what he could, their youth both torturing and soothing him. He would never act on the urge, would not have changed an “F” to a “D” for the momentary succor that the touch of her knifelike legs could have brought him, the swanlike wending angles he would trace with his hands like an antiquarian admiring an especially rare vase. No, he wasn’t that unscrupulous or desperate, and even as he felt age dragging him down, he did not intend to become lecherous. He would never cross that threshold with a student, but there was no harm in crossing it here, alone in the Extended Stay and in his mind. The blaring hum of the air conditioning unit in the corner would drown out those minor moral qualms.

He thrashed in the bed, moribund and miserable. He watched the little sun and rain graphics sprout on the computer-generated America on the TV screen. He was restless, pressured, and had time to kill. The fantasy harmed no one, he told himself, and kissing Emily’s legs and feeling the humid, sticky power of her womanhood as her thighs unlocked usually made good fodder, helped prime him to relieve some tension.

Hotels were perfect places to masturbate, sterile and transient, tended by nonjudgmental clerks who assured patrons that the titles didn’t show up on the bill, maids who had seen worse fluids and who he would never have to meet again, and who didn’t know him in the first place. So why, he asked himself, was it impossible to go through with the rote fantasy tonight? He could usually work his way around the vestiges of Catholic guilt and the professional embarrassment he felt over fantasizing about a student, as long as he told himself beforehand that the health benefits of masturbation, reducing his chance of testicular and prostate cancer, were more than enough reason to be doing this.

Something stopped him tonight, though, and by almost 9 a.m., he thought he knew what that something was: Emily Watterson was only nineteen, a year or two older than Amy Loeher. If he and Janine had been able to conceive, he suddenly realized, his own daughter would have been about Amy's age. He took a pillow in his hand, balled it up and threw it across the bed, cursed himself for having this pang imposed on him at this inopportune moment, this little voice telling him that even in fantasy he would now have to act his age. There were a few secretaries and female professors at the University, so his options for more temperate fodder were still open.

He picked up the cellphone from his nightstand, hit the little telephone icon, and waited while it rang.

"Nebraska Meats, this is Rhonda speaking."

"Hi, Rhonda, my name is James Arklow. I'm a detective. I need to make an inquiry about one of your drivers."

"Hon, I'm just dispatch. I ain't privileged to give out information about drivers." She popped a bubblegum bubble, making the receiver scratch in his ear. He imagined her breath smelled like Juicy Fruit.

"Okay, who would I need to talk to?"

"You want the Skipper."

"Put the Skipper on, please. This is a serious matter."

Rhonda paused for a moment, said nothing. The line went flat, and he feared he might get disconnected. The line rang two more times, a strange anachronistic analogue throwback tone that was probably just used on an in-house basis at the company.

"This is Skip Blaincock. You said you was with the police?"

"This is Detective James Arklow." It was best not to disabuse him of the notion that the police were involved. It was of course illegal to pretend to be an officer, but James saw no harm and quite a bit of percentage in not bothering to correct the Skipper. "Mr. Blaincock, I'm looking for one of your drivers. I'm not sure if he is still hauling for Nebraska Meats, but I believe he was until a few months ago."

"Shoot."

"He's well over six feet tall. He has a beard, long hair. Dark glasses, maybe prescription, maybe not."

"Uh-uh." There was a battle of sounds in the background on Skip's end, a pneumatic piston performing a mating call across a scaffold to a welding torch as it hissed and sparks flew.

"He wears a jacket with a lot of patches and-"

Skip Blaincock laughed, and Detective James Arklow could envision the Cheshire grin that went with that good ole boy cackle, punctuated by a drawn-out hayseed guffaw as the man paused to draw in breath while laughing simultaneously. "Yep, you didn't have to bother with the rest of those pertinent details. We only got one guy gung-ho enough for the firm to wear his company jacket when he's out on the road."

"And who might that be?"

"He goes by the name of Aaron Neblett."

The detective's heart wound a spring tighter. He had a name. "And where is he?"

"I can't tell you where he is right now, but he should be on his way to the Sacramento Sounds headquarters in Sacramento, California." He drawled the state's name out well past its intended number of syllables, twanging it into an expansive phonetic arrangement that he tasted as much as spoke.

"Sacramento Sounds Headquarters?"

"Yep, he's got about a day and a half left before he should touch down there and—"

"Thank you," James said, interrupting Skip and then hanging up on him.

Chapter Fifteen

Something inside of him had cracked, he knew. He had driven the last few-hundred miles covered in dried blood without bothering to change his clothes. The girl sitting in the passenger seat said nothing, but he could hardly blame her. He was a terrifying sight, and she was understandably scared to tell him to change. It was ultimately of very little consequence, since he had an excuse ready for the guard who questioned him at the gate of Sacramento Sounds.

"Yeah, you know," Aaron said, "I don't usually drive these big fancy rigs. I drive refrigerated meat vans. I've been hauling bloody carcasses so long it seeps into all my clothes. I just got done hauling some bison to Bakersfield before coming out here"

"I hear ya," the guard said, and then spoke into the two-way radio clipped to the breast pocket of his uniform. He said something in code to whoever was on the other end of the radio, and then turned his attention back to Aaron in his big rig. "They got a couple of engineers over there with the trailer, so it might be a minute before you take off."

"Okay."

"Just drive straight into the lot and you'll see them back there."

“Right.”

Aaron worked the treadle valve and gas pedal, stab breaking his way forward and giving Amy a minor case of whiplash. She could tell his weird driving maneuvers were unnecessary, that he was merely pissed off and taking it out on his rig, something she had never seen him do. “Does this happen a lot?” She said.

“What?”

“You know, they make you wait?” She expected to feel better when they finally reached their goal, perhaps experiencing some sense of accomplishment. Seeing the men in the white shirts with the work goggles gathered around the trailer, though, she felt only anticlimax. She also expected to see the Pacific Ocean, marine blue waves cresting into frothy white, as gulls dipped low over the heads of exotic palms. Maybe they had come in from the wrong side of town, and the gorgeous view was hidden on the other side of the glass-skinned skyscrapers, but so far Sacramento didn’t have much more to recommend it than Tulsa, Oklahoma.

“Happens all the time. Waiting is in the nature of the beast.” Aaron surprised her by reaching across the gulf between driver and passenger seat to grab a cigarette from the pack of Newports nestled in her purse. She found it odd that he knew exactly where to go in her handbag. She wondered if he knew she had taken one of the condoms filled with dope, without bothering to ask him. If he knew, he betrayed no sign, and might not until it was too late for her, and he was chopping her into bits with his axe and burying her in a sandpit at some lonely runaway truck ramp, on some desolate stretch of highway.

Amy suppressed a shiver as a chill went through her body, and she listened to him as he spoke. "A lot of the time when you pull into a lot, it's near the end of the load crew's shift. So they spend an hour or so bullshitting on the dock. That way the next guys coming on get shafted with the unloading job. But that's clearly not what's going on here."

He pointed through the dirty windshield at the men who were doing circuit tracing on wires inside the tractor that Aaron was tasked to pull. The belly boxes on the massive Sacramento Sounds trailer were deployed, and the dolly legs were mated to their plates on the concrete ground beneath them. One of the engineers finally noticed Aaron and Amy sitting in their big rig. He set down his wire diagram and came over to the driver's side of the truck. He wore a sweat-soaked blue baseball cap.

"It looks like we're having a wiring problem with the expandable show trailer. Can't get the hydraulic shocks to respond either."

"That's too bad," Aaron said. "You know when you might have her online and running?"

The man took off his hat, scratched his scalp, and whistled out a stream of hot air. "At the latest, sometime early tomorrow morning I'd say.

That's if we have to go to distribution to get parts. We're still troubleshooting right now."

"Fuck." Aaron took a pack of matches from his pocket he'd picked up at a restaurant called "Buckhorn Exchange." He struck one and lit his cigarette with a flourish. The engineer looked like he wanted to say something about smoking around his precious high-end toys. The way Aaron saw it, the egghead was clearly not in a position to dictate to anyone, considering he couldn't even get his million dollar junk heap to function.

Aaron didn't so much puff the cigarette as drink a third of the papered tobacco in one rush of anger. He checked himself, struggled against the desire to blow smoke directly into Pencil Neck's face, and said instead, "You mind if we stay in the yard overnight, if it takes that long?"

The engineer replaced his ball cap on his head. "No, that would actually be better for us. I mean you could go shack up in a motel. There's a Radisson up the street. But the fact of the matter is it could be another five minutes, or it could be another twelve hours. But we'll have you a seaworthy vessel ready in good time."

He winked. Aaron didn't wink back. Instead, he drew his cigarette down to the filter, until his fingers burned. He flicked his butt into the lot and said, as much to no one as to the engineer, "I'm going to go take a shower." He half-stood, walked through the bamboo bead curtain.

"I hope you're decent!"

"I am," Amy said.

She had just finished changing. She had shed the butterfly print sundress and exchanged it for a feathered skirt, its lower half made from synthetic rayon that was supposed to resemble black boa feathers. It was an unseasonably short dress, something befitting a kind of morbid ball for gothic debutantes, or more appropriate for a young widow on prom night, than the kind of tomboy apparel one would normal expect from woman riding shotgun in this kind of rig. It was strapless, the top half of the dress a cinched mass of ruffled black silk that collected what little fat there was around her pale breasts.

Aaron laughed, seeming to get a kick out of it. "California's warm, girl, but it ain't warm enough for something that skimpy."

"I'm not worried about the weather. I'll stay in the sleeper."

"Well, you might as well. We're not going anywhere."

"Really?"

Aaron nodded. "We'll probably be here overnight. So do me a favor."

"Sure."

"Go chock the wheels. I don't want to set the brakes when she's running this hot. Lock the fuel cap, too."

"Why the fuel cap?" She wedged her feet into leather thong sandals as she spoke.

"I don't want some joker sneaking into the lot at night and putting something in the fuel tank.

It's happened to me before." He grabbed the front door of the bathroom, declared, "I'm taking a shower." He closed the door behind himself and disrobed, his clothes still caked with the blood of the two Arapahoe boys he buried back there on the Res. He turned on the hot and cold taps, which seemed to hold better water pressure when the vehicle was at rest.

He placed himself beneath the showerhead, gripping the exposed pipe like a snake charmer handling his pet cobra, letting the strong, scalding nettles of fresh water envelope him in a steam that took away the stress of the last few days, and the frustrations of the last hour. Afterwards, he changed into a white terrycloth bathrobe he took from some hotel on one of his many cross-country journeys.

The shag carpet of the sleeper dried the moisture beading off his feet as he crossed the short threshold from the berth to the front of the truck. He found Amy sprawled in the passenger seat, reposed as if the rig were her glorified barcalounger. She was painting her toenails a strawberry shade while listening to the usual useless blather on the Cobra radio.

"You got your GPS," a nasal voice was saying, clearly in the heat of a litany whose opening stanzas Aaron was grateful to have missed. "Then you got the infrared devices that watch you all day. I'm talking your Easy Pass, your Pre-Pass, a whole plethora of engine signatures, cameras, x-ray machines at the border checkpoints."

"'A plethora of engine signatures,'" Aaron sneered.

"He's worrying me," Amy said.

"You shouldn't worry. Old boy's full of shit."

"And these devices are tracking everything you do, from your speed, to your location, the elevation, your direction. You got to pay attention." Amy leaned forward, adjusted the volume upward, a credulous look of worry furrowing her brow. "Take heed of light poles, overpasses, at intersections. Always look at the chicken coops and the Evil Knievels."

"What are Evil Knievels and chicken coops?" Amy asked.

"Evil Knievels are your motorcycle cops. Chicken coops are your weigh stations."

"Oh."

"Guy's a blowhard." Aaron reached out to shut his CB radio off. "He has this little theory you can throw your Qualcomm off by putting tinfoil over the antenna."

"What's the Qualcomm?"

Aaron tapped the screen of his little onboard computer. Amy pointed her lacquer-covered toenail brush at the screen, coming perilously close to getting red polish on it. "What are those little square dot things?"

"Rest areas."

"And the things that say 'alt?'"

Aaron yawned, stretched out in his seat luxuriously. "Those are alternate routes. They're usually scenic. They go through landmarks. They can be right beautiful, but we don't have the spare time for any of that noise right now."

"Oh." Amy pulled her foot toward her face, blew on her toes in an effort to make the acrylic dry faster. She would have asked Aaron to blow on them, knew that most men would have jumped at the opportunity, but she knew he didn't swing that way. She was grateful that his fetishes kept his attention turned elsewhere. This trip would have been a bigger nightmare if she had been forced to fend off the octopus-like advances of some horny bastard who couldn't keep his hands off her. She was on the verge of declaring to herself that Aaron Neblett was somehow growing on her, but she held off on making that affirmation (even silently and to herself) for fear of what it might mean.

"Here." Aaron adjusted a couple of knobs among the gathered array of instrument clusters on the glowing panel. Heat poured through the vents. "Put your feet up there. It's more comfortable than bending yourself all out of shape, and they'll dry faster."

"Thanks."

They remained quiet for a moment, gazed through the front windshield at the granite bone yard stretching out in front of them. The terminal was at the foot of the Tower Bridge, catching golden light from the sun as it broke through the steel beams, forming a radiant unbroken sheen across the rippling aureate surface of the glasslike water, and throwing a commensurate black shadow across the concrete basin below.

"It's beautiful," Amy said.

"You ain't just whistling 'Dixie.'" Aaron folded his hands behind his head. If he had a cold Bud Light in his left hand and Chocolate Thunder's cock in his right, he could have died happy at that moment. Amy, sensing the revivifying effect of his shower, decided to have her nightcap in the front of the cab rather than going back to the sleeper to snort her bump. The engineers were still busy struggling with their trailer, and would be none the wiser. Some dim instinct told her Aaron was past caring, and that there would be no consequences for violating his rule. His ban on smoking was also apparently no longer an edict either.

Amy used the gas key she took off the chain dangling from the ignition when she had gone around the tractor locking up the gas tanks as Aaron asked her to do. She dipped it into the cocaine-saturated condom, lifted the small pile of powder to her nose, and pulled until her left ear twitched, as if on a string. Aaron hummed "White Christmas" next to her, perhaps ironically, with his eyes closed and his deep breaths coming like the slow laboring gusts of a fireplace bellows. Amy knew him well enough to know that in a moment he would be snoring.

She sucked the key with her tongue, fellating the tiny piece of metal until the inside of her mouth was numb enough to take an icicle to the roof without her wincing. Then she reattached the key to the chain dangling from the steering column. She dug a cigarette out of her vinyl purse, and lit up with a miniature Bic lighter adorned with a bald eagle clutching an American flag in its talons. She smoked, and blew the smoke across her newly-shellacked toes.

"I forgot to ask you," she said, banking on the possibility that Aaron had yet to fall asleep.

"Mm?"

"Where did you get this stuff? It's so fucking good."

Aaron grinned, scratched his beard, which was coarse enough for the sound to resemble a Brillo pad rubbing against sandpaper. "Santa Claus," he said, and resumed humming "White Christmas" in a laconic Bing Crosby baritone. "I got it from Santa Claus." Then he slept. Amy followed him into slumber shortly thereafter, the powder coursing through her brain finally relenting, as her too tired body dropped off into a quiet, curtained-off stasis on the other side of dreamland.

Several hundred miles to their south, Detective James Arklow drove while they slept, cursing the big liquid tanker truck with its elliptical fuel payload which blocked the right lane. Another smoothbore biohazard tanker kept him from getting around the other truck, both of them hogging the road in tandem, as if it was a conspiracy to deny the insignificant little four-doors their passage on the highway.

No sooner did he finally find a narrow alley to escape from between the two trucks, then did the vacationers begin to show up in force, driving slowly in their campers with banana-yellow kayaks moored to their roofs and the Golden Retrievers catching air with their lolling tongues while they stuck their heads out of windows and dripped wet bands of saliva onto the hood of the detective's passing sedan.

He drove so fast, so well in excess of the speed limit that it was almost as if God or nature could not keep up with him, and threw weather out in a schizophrenic pattern that changed as the rollercoaster elevation dipped and rose. He climbed three-thousand feet as quickly as he ever had, faster than when he had driven from Flagstaff to Phoenix to attend a symposium on the ethics of investigative surveillance, going from ice-cold pine country to a land of parched cactus in the time it took an AM radio preacher to segue from hellfire to salvation. He was pelted by hale one moment, and chastised by heat the very next. If the sun shining during a thunderstorm meant the devil was beating his wife, then this weather spoke of a case of domestic violence in hell so brutal that it now required some kind of divine intercession.

His panic increased with the elevation, the mountain ranges depriving him of whatever oxygen he hadn't lost worrying over Amy and what might become of her in the next few hours.

Chapter Sixteen

Sunrise broke over the Central California Valley in a wash of red and orange clouds that receded by the time Aaron and Amy woke up, leaving the sky an unbroken shade of blue which held no memory of the earlier array of colors, and seemed to stretch toward the four corners of the horizon into infinity.

Aaron gave Amy a little barefoot nudge to wake her, and then he went into the sleeping berth. He changed out of his bathrobe into a set of work clothes. He found Amy sitting up when he returned to the cab. She held her legs to her chest, and was curled into a fetal ball. Her black feather dress was crumpled, and she wore a cranky expression as she smoked her morning menthol. She stared out through the windshield.

"Did they ever get the trailer fixed?"

"Well, I aim to go out there in a couple of minutes and find out."

None of the engineers seemed to be milling around outside of their cab. Some yard hostler fairy had apparently lifted the dolly legs out of their plates during the night, and returned the hand crank to its traveling case. Aaron figured it even money that the expandable show trailer (built by the same genius that designed the Budweiser Hydroplane) would be ready for the road soon.

He stole the still-burning cigarette from Amy's hand and puffed. "You still want to be a truck driver?"

"I don't know," she said, snapping the fingers of her left hand and demanding that he replace the cigarette he had stolen.

He was not quite ready to give it up, however, and took another couple of puffs. "Yeah, it's got its upsides and its downsides. If you get as little as two moving violations in three years, they're liable to cancel your insurance or jack the rates up so high that if you so much as fart or cough one more time, you're off the road."

Amy gave up on getting her cigarette back. She took another one out of her pack, lit it, and listened to him as he spoke. "If you get too used to driving a big rig like this one, it gets to the point where you can't even drive a real car anymore. They're too small, and they handle too different for me to get the hang of them again." He gripped the steering wheel as if he would be moored to it forever, doomed to drive a slab of meat from Nebraska to El Paso, over and over again.

"Still it's hard to beat making twenty-eight cents a mile." He finished his cigarette and threw it out the driver's side window. He was about to say something else when his phone rang, dancing as it shook in the cup holder on vibrate. He glanced once at the face of the cell phone, and answered. "Rhonda, I was just about to call."

"Tell me you made it," she said, smacking the last of her gum's flavor into her taste buds as she spoke.

"Honey, I made it with bells on. Driver two-six-seven is here standing tall before the man."

"Thanks, hon." Rhonda was about to hang up, but added as an afterthought, "Oh, you seem to be getting pretty popular around here. There's a guy who called looking-"

"Sir?" An arm bearing a clipboard reached through the driver's side window. It was a yard hostler wearing a blue Chino shirt with a laminated nametag that said "Chet" clipped below a sew-on patch which read "Sacramento Sounds" in florid cursive.

"Rhonda," Aaron said, "I got to let you go." He hung up the phone and took the clipboard from the kid. He signed the bill of lading, skipping from field to field with the ballpoint pen anchored to the clipboard by a small chain. He looked down at the young yard hostler. "They about ready to go?"

"You're clear to couple up," the kid said.

"Good deal," Aaron said, and opened his door. The kid stepped back, and Aaron hopped down. He stretched, basked in the warm breeze carrying across the blacktop of the terminal yard. The smell of hot tar reminded him of days spent on grade school playgrounds as a child, and the cruel lessons meted out there. "Let me get a battle plan drawn up here," Aaron said.

The kid followed him around behind the massive Sacramento Sounds trailer, where Aaron used his hands like an auteur filmmaker on location trying to frame a shot. He visualized it all in his head, how the fifth wheel apron would mate and lock with the kingpin on down to how he would minimize jacking and get the rig on out of here. "Most accidents happen when you're backing up." The hostler nodded at the sage advice of the old war dog.

"Nice mud flaps," Aaron said, admiring the twin depictions of Yosemite Sam holding a couple of six shooters and announcing "Back Off!" to any tailgating varmint who had a mind to ride the rig too close.

Returning to his own rig, he noticed bits of what appeared to be bloody suet leaking from the wheel well. Looking at the hot concrete beneath the truck, he saw the decapitated body of a Yellow Headed Collared lizard, its dry skin crinkling as it ceased to camouflage itself, and resolved its scaly hide to assume a nondescript dirty brown shade it would wear into the ground.

"Poor bastard," Aaron said. The yard hostler stood next to him, and they both grimaced at the remains of the lizard. "I probably clocked the little fella somewhere in Nevada. Or maybe I did it in Colorado."

Inside of the truck, Amy greeted the day with her own variation on the requisite cup of morning Joe. Coke, she discovered some time ago, was quite the eye-opener. She turned the condom inside out, and stuffed it into her nostril as if it was a new nasal decongestant she just invented.

She no longer tasted her bad breath, felt as if someone placed a sliver of wintergreen mint beneath her tongue. The sun was no longer harsh or hot. It was more like butter or gold leaking through, making a glorious stained glass relief on the previously dirty windshield. "California," she said. "I love you."

Maybe she could get Aaron to take her to the ocean. She had never seen the beach before. She removed the distended balloon from her nose, crumpled it into a ball, and threw it out of the window. A loud pop jolted her, something like a car backfiring, followed by a string of firecrackers going off. The reports traded, until she realized what it actually was.

It was a sound familiar from those long nights where she lay awake in the third floor of her Kroc Houses apartment. It was a sound whose origin could no longer be doubted or questioned when it ripped a hole through the tractor, punching through the driver's side door and landing in the steering column.

"Shit!" She dropped to the floorboards, plugged her ears as the two dueling .38s took potshots, the sonic blast of the heavier Taurus replying two or three times to the lighter air-weight. Amy opened the passenger door and fell onto the concrete, scraping her left elbow and right knee as she struggled behind the front right wheel, crouching there.

Directly in front of her she saw the yard hostler, lying on his back. His mouth was open, forming a smaller dark hole to go with the large one he now wore on his forehead. "Amy." The voice was strange, new and weak. She had never heard him so soft, helpless, crying out to her. She looked toward the sound, saw Aaron on the other side of the truck, lying in a pile. His steel-toed work boots kicked the air, searching with the paralyzed grasp of a dying insect's feelers. The cylinder of his Taurus .38 revolver was open in his left hand, empty and smoking. A pile of spent brass was collected in a pile next to him.

"Ah." He tried to say her name again and got a mouthful of blood for his troubles. She crawled toward him, sliding underneath the truck, keeping a low profile to avoid the steaming muffler, the drip of undefined fluids, heated and smelling of noxious chemicals as they poured, the little bits of luminescent glass cutting her as she shimmied forward.

Aaron's eyes widened, as if she were the light at the end of a tunnel, a boyhood dog returning to his arms across the chasm of time, now that he was dying and about to be reunited with his loved ones among the stars, redeemed and cleansed of all his sorrow and past crimes, those seemingly empty gestures in the pews of the nondenominational chapels in the truck stops now justified, if only this little winged white angel would take him into her arms and they could ascend together.

She ignored his outstretched hand, placed her fingers around his throat as if searching for a pulse. She reached for his neckline and pulled, removing the dog tag chain that held the special little key.

It dawned on him what she wanted, and he struggled against the mouthful of blood to speak again, this time forming very different words from the ones previously prepared. He died before he could speak again, and rolled onto his back to face the sun. It ended for him while he stared up into the sky.

Amy rolled right, cutting her thighs, cursing the short dress she wore. Once free of the undercarriage, she hopped back into the truck and grabbed her purse.

She broke through the bamboo-beaded curtain one last time, searching the sleeper berth for her effects, gathering up lighters, matches, toiletries, and stuffing them into her purse. Then she walked back to the front of the truck and hopped down, ignoring all of the dead man's previous advice about maintaining "three points of contact" when exiting or entering the truck.

She was not sure how she felt about his death, whether it was good or bad. She knew only that it meant she was free, free perhaps to start her own life, or to abandon the same to the will of the pimp who called himself God.

For a brief moment she contemplated searching Aaron Neblett's body for the few thousand dollars he had on him, but she decided against it. She wanted now only to go. She walked around to the back of the tractor, hopped up, and inserted the key into the headache rack. She opened it slowly, letting the metal face fall forward. She unstrapped the First Aid kit from the Velcro rack and carefully lowered it from the cab guard. She looked inside, saw the translucent sleeves packed with driven snow. There was a lot in there, she knew, enough to make the present time stretch into a blissful trance state that would keep the past buried and the future delayed for as long as possible.

She imagined she could get a good hotel suite with quality room service, enjoy a week or two of warm Jacuzzi baths, hot fudge sundaes, and cocaine. Maybe she would call Conchita, if she was still alive and still working the hoe stroll.

"Amy Loeher?"

She closed the First Aid kit, and quickly turned. "Yeah?"

It was a man, well-past middle age. He had a gut with the dimension of a queen-sized pillow stuffed underneath his blue button-down Oxford shirt. His eyes were two steel pits, the irises the size of Pimento olives, but planted in a face of ruddy clay the size of a Bull Mastiff's head. The man's expression was hard, but not cruel. Amy read people well, men better than women, and she knew instantly that he had seen far more evil than he had done.

"My name is Detective James Arklow. Your mother, Margaret Loeher, sent me to save you."

"Save me? You mean like Jesus?"

The detective replaced his air-weight pistol in its holster. "Well, not exactly."

"Like a prince who saves a princess from a dragon? Something like that?"

"More like that. Maybe I should have said she sent me to find you, not save you."

"You found me," Amy said, lifting her purse in one hand, and her metal box in the other, in a gesture of defiance. "Are you going to arrest me?"

"No." His face reddened. He wiped the sweat from his forehead, cleared the moisture from the perplexed mask of confusion he wore. "I'm a private detective. You're not in trouble. Your mother just wanted—"

This second mention of her mother made Amy Loeher coil like a snake preparing to strike. "My mother? That bitch called the police on me, reported me for running away. And now she wants me back?"

The detective shook his head, thinking that the girl misunderstood, that he perhaps failed to explain the situation coherently, and that everything could be righted if he just found another way to phrase it. "Your mom just wants to know you're okay."

"Okay, then. Then tell my mom I'm okay. And tell her a couple of other things, too, all right?"

"All right."

"Tell her I'm eighteen. That means I'm an adult. Tell her that I'm a whore, too. Can you do that for me?"

The detective looked down at his loafers, wiped the pile of his thinning hair from his forehead.

"And tell her one more thing, okay? Tell her I've moved to California. And I'm going to stay here until I die."

Amy turned, and marched for the open gate of the terminal yard. Downtown Sacramento beckoned beyond the gates, the midday sun turning the streets into a blast furnace, smelting the sidewalks and burning the feathers on the birds as they flitted over the parked cars and people walking in the city below them.

The detective wanted to chase her, but knew he had to stay at the crime scene until the cops came. He looked toward the truck. The box at the back of the rig was open, displaying a case the girl had raided, leaving an exposed axe whose head was covered with dried blood and gristle. James Arklow walked forward to get a better look at the axe, pulled his cellphone from his pocket, and dialed Margaret Loeher to give her the good news.

Chapter Seventeen

An ambuscade of gray snow fell from the dark clouds hovering above the sleepy campus. It was too much to hope for a pristine blizzard, what with the crosscurrents from the paper mill to the west and the rendering plant off to the east both meeting at the technical college, causing Professor Arklow to cough once before he even had a chance to take a drag on his cigarette. His department chair, Les Forman, stood with him on one of the two gazebos on campus, and guarded James from the wind until he managed to get his cigarette lit.

"Thanks, Les." Professor Arklow stuck his free hand into the bubbly pocket of his goose down jacket, and shivered while he smoked.

Les dug, with trembling hands, into his own pack of smokes and extracted a Marlboro light. Les was the only other person on campus to Professor Arklow's knowledge who had ever served in the military or been on the police force, or openly voted Republican in the last twenty years. As a result, both men were regarded by most of the other professors as potential adherents to the philosophy of either Benito Mussolini or Adolph Hitler, and conceivably both. In truth, however, they had given up on politics altogether, but now bonded in the mutual conspiracy of their indifference to any conceit besides giving the other professors a target to hate.

"Well," James said, puffing his cigarette. "I guess I'm a smoker again."

"What makes you say that, Inspector Poirot? The cigarette in your hand?"

James smiled. He stared at the distant parking lot, near Woodward Hall. His car was blanketed in a dirty off-white powder at least three inches thick, his windshield wipers hidden beneath the snow that continued to accumulate. He could vaguely discern the form of a custodian in the distance, who was laying down a sheet of rock salt as he blinkered in and out of view.

"No," Professor Arklow said, finally. "It's just I told myself that I was going to have a few cigarettes to take the edge off, to help me transition back from sabbatical."

"Grading their term papers is enough to make anyone take up the habit. Christ, heroin couldn't numb the pain I felt after reading that last batch." Les pulled the sheep's wool ears down on his lumberjack hat and stamped his feet in place.

"Yeah, but considering I'm out here freezing my balls off, I think I've got to face the fact that I'm really a smoker again." He flicked the butt off the gazebo and it landed silently in the mounting pile of accumulated snow. He stepped in each one of the already-formed footprints that he made coming out here, and he headed back down the salt-caked sidewalk, toward his office. The windows of the brick buildings at the four corners of the quad glowed with a buttery light that promised warmth, and made him walk double-time toward Porter Hall, where his office was.

"I'm freezing my balls off too!" Les Forman's voice rang out behind him. James did not turn around. *Freezing my balls off,* he thought, and wondered what kind of effect cigarettes had on his sperm and their motility. He was contemplating going to a clinic, getting checked out again, maybe seeing if it wasn't too late to do all of the holistic stuff the doctor had told him about, the things he didn't want to hear about when he was with Janine, but which might be worth checking out if he and Diane ever got serious. A small part of him still wanted to be a father, and it wasn't too late.

He and Diane had met under the worst of circumstances, or at least he regarded them as such. About a month after the unsatisfying conclusion of the Amy Loeher case, he had decided to write an article for potential submission to *Private Investigator Monthly.* He had begun it in order to help distract him from his abiding belief that he had failed, in life in general, and on the case in particular. He had told Maggie Loeher that her daughter was alive, which was all she had wanted, really, but that somehow still was not enough.

Amy wasn't dead at the bottom of the lake, and her head was not one of the six trophies recovered from Aaron Neblett's freezer by the North Platte Police Department, but James knew that things were not likely to end well for her, either.

He wrote about these feelings, the various scenarios he imagined for Amy, of her working in a bottomless joint not unlike the "Bare Sensations" strip club her mother had mentioned, of her perhaps overdosing at some point in the near-future, or still selling her body for someone like God Body Divine. Maybe she had already returned to her old pimp. James had contemplated visiting the McDonald's franchisee more than once, but resisted the urge for fear of what he might do to the man when he saw him again.

He tied his feelings about the Loeher case to other unresolved echoes of cases from his time on the Force, and under the tentative title of "When the Princess is the Dragon," he asked the readership composed of other PIs if in fact some people did not want to be saved or found, and if that was not in fact their right, despite the pain their absence caused their loved ones. Amy, after all, was an adult in the legal sense, if in no other.

He had finished the article, asked Les for a second set of eyes, and got his department chair's seal-of-approval, before sending it off to *PIM.* The magazine had a response time of six-to-eight weeks, which gave him plenty of time to fret, to doubt and to praise himself, to envision the acceptance letter as it arrived in a self-addressed stamped envelope with a handwritten congratulatory note. He graded his students' papers while he waited, read their three-to-five pages double spaced essays on sentencing disparities based on the socioeconomic background of murderers, and the fate of his editorial began in his mind to gather an importance beyond anything he had ever ascribed to any of his cases, or to his entire career.

It was madness, all out of proportion to reality, he knew, but nothing could stop him from running to his faculty mail cubby several times a day, like a rat pressing the lever in its Skinner box.

His SASE finally came back to him at the end of the eighth week, a good omen, he told himself. All of his rejections had gone through the turnaround process in six weeks flat. James tore the seal on the envelope, his hand trembling so badly that the pages of his paper-clipped article scattered to the ground, along with a handwritten note.

He saw the ballpoint pen strokes on the small leaf of red paper, no heavier than toilet tissue or the receipt at an all-night diner. He picked the note up, and read the florid script written in heavy, blue stains: "TOO BLEAK. Review our editorial guidelines."

On his lunch break that afternoon, the failed editorialist went to a convenience store and bought a pack of Virginia Slim 100s and a candy bar, neither of which did much for his diabetes. He smoked the cigarette and chewed the candy bar, holding the Slim in his right hand and the nougat bar in his left. He heard the specter of George Bernard Shaw in his ear, whispering about how those who couldn't do, taught. And further, that those who couldn't teach, ended up teaching at Fairborn Tech.

It had occurred to him as he ate and smoked that the Virginias were something he never would have bought back when he was a real smoker, that it was his way of sharing some kind of communion with Margaret Loeher, who he had never had the nerve to call again after that final message he gave her in the parking lot of Sacramento Sounds, where he stared at that gristle-laden axe which was casting an ever-lengthening shadow across his dreams these days.

A week after getting his rejection slip, he had gotten an e-mail from Diane. The message said she was junior editor at *Private Investigator Monthly*, and that furthermore she had recently been fired from the magazine over creative differences with the senior staff. They had clashed repeatedly regarding which stories to include and which to reject.

After an especially heated argument, she tendered her resignation, and began scouring the slush pile, looking for the seed of a story good enough to be fleshed out into the flagship book of the True Crime imprint she wanted to start. She was convinced after much searching that she had found her author and her story, in Detective

James Arklow and his tale of the Amy Loeher disappearance.

They had corresponded via e-mail several times, and then began talking on the telephone. They were tentatively scheduled to meet at the Private Investigation Technology Conference at a hotel in Dallas in two weeks' time. James had briefly contemplated writing an article on the use of social media sites in solving cases for *PIM,* but it was a subject that had already been done to death, he knew. Besides, he had begun to concentrate on the tenuous outline of the book he wanted to write for Diane and her fledgling imprint.

He also had a suspicion, however tenuous, that they might actually hit it off when they met. Her name on the *PIM* website masthead linked to her CV online, which featured a headshot. The image was small, but she was clearly attractive, with black hair, dark eyes, and vaguely Sicilian features. She was ten years his junior, but still older than most of his students, which meant she was not young enough to get the punks or the busybody faculty members talking about how unscrupulous of a cradle robber he was, if indeed he ever brought her on campus.

He wasn't expecting her hand in marriage, but anything, ultimately, was possible. Anything was also preferable to the loneliness he felt crowding in on him now.

He walked back into his office and sat down in his swivel chair. He had forgotten to close his door, and now had a view of Dr. Chloe Leachman's office directly across the hall. She was a tenured Humanities professor whose devotion to stealing office supplies was matched only by her penchant for cats. Several stuffed animal Garfield cats were suctioned to the windows of her office, blotting out any passerby's view of the mountain of copier paper she had taken from the supply room. There were several Valentine's Day and Mother's Day plush novelty kittens perched atop her filing cabinets, cradling fury hearts and satin cupid arrows, and there were two posters adorning her front door, one of an anthropomorphic kitten holding a sniper rifle, and the other a classic motivational poster of a cat grasping a tree branch. "Hang in there, kitty."

James spun in his swivel chair, removed his goose down jacket, and hung it on the back of his seat. He stared out the window, at the campus turned a somber blue under the force of the snow. He took a red pen from on top of his desk, and he took the topmost essay from the stack of ungraded papers. The title was "Jim Crow 2.0: Sentence Disparities among the Races." It had been written by one of his few students capable of both expressing a cogent thought and using MLA format for citation.

He was three sentences into reading the paper when a mild flapping noise, followed by a light wind, caused him to spin back around. He and the mailman locked eyes. "Ah," the mailman said. "Here."

He held out a manila envelope. James accepted it in his hand. “Thank you.” The mailman disappeared, the sound of his wallet chain clanking link by link as he faded away down the hall.

Professor Arklow looked at the envelope. Very little mail came to him here, usually just rejection letters from the magazine, and the occasional premature and unwanted article from the AARP. The return address on the envelope was Maggie Loeher’s place on Boniface. He opened the manila package so quickly that he feared he had torn whatever was inside. When he finally shed the paper he saw that the envelope contained a sturdy mortarboard, which he then flipped open.

On top of a watermarked certificate of some kind, someone had taped a small note, a sheet of paper from a pad no larger than the kind he carried with him when he did field work on investigations. This loose leaf might have even been from one of his notebooks, for all he knew. “She wanted me to give this to you,” Margaret Loeher had scribbled in soft graphite. James pulled the taped note away from the matted sheet, which said:

> THIS CERTIFIES THAT AMY LOEHER HAS BEEN FOUND WORTHY IN CHARACTER AND CITIZENSHIP AND HAS SATISFACTORILY COMPLETED THE COURSE OF STUDY IN ACCORDANCE WITH THE GENERAL EQUIVALENCY PROGRAM OF THE STATE

James closed the mortarboard before he could finish reading, and he set it on top of the stack of ungraded papers. He stood up out of his swivel chair and walked to his door, which he closed and then locked. He turned off the lights in his office, and a moment after the sickly fluorescence was gone, the icy blue light from outside of the window took on a soft glow. The snow wasn't ugly anymore. It was easy in the dark to pretend he was not at some nowhere technical college in the Midwest, where he was stuck teaching to students who weren't much more interested in the subject than he was, where they pretended in order to get their credits, and he pretended in order to get paid.

He closed his eyes for a moment, heaved a massive sigh, and realized when he opened his eyes again that, despite his best efforts, he was going to break his streak and cry for the first time in at least a decade.

PUBLISHER'S NOTE

Now that you have finished reading this book, the author would be most grateful if you would take the time to post an honest review of it on Amazon, Barnes & Noble or any other online bookseller's web site.

Anyone with an Amazon account can post reviews, even if you purchased the book somewhere else. If you ever purchased anything on Amazon, you have an account. Your review need not be long. A fair, objective and authentic review is requested so others may benefit from your opinion. It need not be long, just a couple of well chosen sentences can be enough to help potential readers decide if the book is worth their time. Your opinion is valuable to both the author and the publisher.

The author-publisher team put a lot of effort into editing the manuscript before publication, but no book is perfect. If you notice an error, you could help improve future editions by emailing us with page number and line so it can be corrected.

Finally, if you enjoyed the book, be sure to tell your friends about it, in person and on social media such as Facebook, Twitter, LinkedIn and others.

Gene D. Robinson
publisher@moonshinecovepublishing.com

CPSIA information can be obtained at www.ICGtesting.com
Printed in the USA
BVOW01s1600130914

366631BV00003B/245/P

9 781937 327255